CRAFTING

⌒ *for* ⌒

MURDER

A Gasper's Cove Cozy Mystery

BARBARA EMODI

C&T PUBLISHING
Another Maker Inspired!

Text copyright © 2023 by Barbara Emodi

Artwork copyright ©2023 by C&T Publishing, Inc.

Publisher: Amy Barrett-Daffin

Creative Director: Gailen Runge

Senior Editor: Roxane Cerda

Cover Designer: Mariah Sinclair

Book Designer: April Mostek

Production Coordinator: Zinnia Heinzmann

Illustrator: Emilija Mihajlov

Published by C&T Publishing, Inc., P.O. Box 1456, Lafayette, CA 94549

All rights reserved. No part of this work covered by the copyright hereon may be used in any form or reproduced by any means—graphic, electronic, or mechanical, including photocopying, recording, taping, or information storage and retrieval systems—without written permission from the publisher. The copyrights on individual artworks are retained by the artists as noted in *Crafting for Murder*. These designs may be used to make items for personal use only and may not be used for the purpose of personal profit. Items created to benefit nonprofit groups, or that will be publicly displayed, must be conspicuously labeled with the following credit: "Designs copyright © 2023 by Barbara Emodi from the book *Crafting for Murder* from C&T Publishing, Inc." Permission for all other purposes must be requested in writing from C&T Publishing, Inc.

Attention Teachers: C&T Publishing, Inc., encourages the use of our books as texts for teaching. You can find lesson plans for many of our titles at ctpub.com or contact us at ctinfo@ctpub.com.

We take great care to ensure that the information included in our products is accurate and presented in good faith, but no warranty is provided, nor are results guaranteed. Having no control over the choices of materials or procedures used, neither the author nor C&T Publishing, Inc., shall have any liability to any person or entity with respect to any loss or damage caused directly or indirectly by the information contained in this book. For your convenience, we post an up-to-date listing of corrections on our website (ctpub.com). If a correction is not already noted, please contact our customer service department at ctinfo@ctpub.com or P.O. Box 1456, Lafayette, CA 94549.

Trademark (™) and registered trademark (®) names are used throughout this book. Rather than use the symbols with every occurrence of a trademark or registered trademark name, we are using the names only in the editorial fashion and to the benefit of the owner, with no intention of infringement.

Library of Congress Control Number: 2022921536

Printed in the USA

10 9 8 7 6 5 4 3 2 1

DEDICATION

*For Scarlett MacDonald writer, editor,
and friend of these characters.*

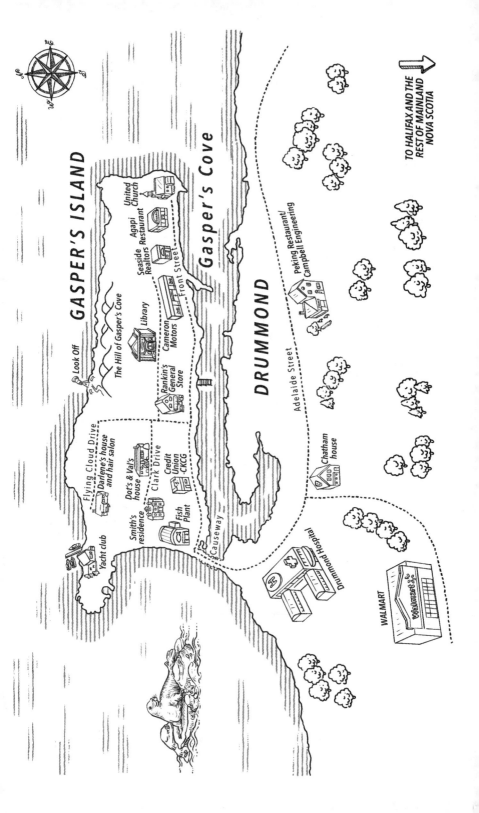

CHAPTER ONE

Gerry Richards, CKGC Gasper's Cove Radio's "Voice of the Waves," spoke into the mic, but his eyes were on me.

"Valerie Rankin, are you saying you tricked the province into believing in a business that doesn't exist, selling merchandise you don't really have?"

He sat back and waited.

The roots of my hair prickled, hot under the tight leatherette headset. The tiny wood-paneled room closed in on me. It smelled of Old Spice and burnt coffee. The last time I'd been in a radio station I was working as a night cleaner at the Canadian Broadcasting Corporation offices in Halifax, Nova Scotia's capital. When my neighbor said he could set up an interview because the announcer owed him rent, he didn't tell me it was going to be this hard.

"Gerry, it's not the way it sounds. The Department of Tourism wanted businesses owned by women for the *Out and About* guide. I went online and applied. Wasn't expecting to hear back, to be honest." Had this man never had nothing to lose? Never done anything on impulse?

"You told them about a grand opening of some kind of crafters' co-op, am I right?" Gerry was awfully smug for a man in a one-room radio station above the credit union on Front Street, in an office chair missing one wheel, duct tape holding it all together.

"Look. This is rural Nova Scotia," I said. "All I want is to get crafts out of people's houses and into a central location." How hard could it be? Besides, if I couldn't get something organized here soon, it would be back to the city and the dead-end jobs I'd done most of my working life. I couldn't let that happen. "Everyone in Gasper's Cove makes something. It's all there is to do, now the fishery's slowed down. We knit, crochet, carve, sew, make pots and jewelry." I looked up at the foam egg cartons stapled to the ceiling. I was sure Gerry had done that himself.

Gerry leaned toward me, his pilled fleece vest zipped and straining over a worn poly/cotton shirt. As a garment sewer, I knew this was a tough body to dress well. Gerry wasn't even trying.

"Where's this co-op of yours, this consignment shop thing, located?"

"It's not exactly *located* yet, Gerry. We're in the process of setting it up on the second floor of our store—you know, Rankin's General, down the street."

"Not ready?" Gerry let his rich baritone linger, letting the folks at home appreciate the gravity of my situation.

"The space will be ready. No problem," I said. "We've just got to clean it up a bit and start collecting crafts."

"How do you propose to do that?" Gerry asked.

"I've told my sewing students to spread the word," I said, catching Gerry's smirk at the mention of what, to him, was a mundane, female activity. "We've put up notices around town, and I thought anyone listening can contact me." The next part I'd rehearsed. Speaking slowly and carefully, I recited my cell phone number and email address and asked anyone interested to drop off samples at the store.

It was a relief when Gerry turned from me to his mic, raised a finger for me to wait, listened to something only he could hear, and flicked a switch. The faint beat of the "Guess Who" echoed in the room.

I was done.

Sliding his headset off and down his neck, Gerry reached for mine. "Had the warden in earlier. He's got a bigger head than you, in more ways than one. Had to adjust this. First time doing radio?" he asked, as he leaned into me, brushing his hands over my hair as he freed me from the earphones. He'd had bacon and onions for lunch.

Of course, the town warden, what the mayor was called in small communities like ours. I tried to keep steady in my own tippy chair. "I've been in studios before, but only behind the scenes."

"Thought so. Got to do these community-interest spots, but investigative journalism is more my beat. Plus, I've got a face for radio." Gerry laughed, enjoying the worn joke. "I send my assistant, young Noah, out to do the human-interest stuff. He's off now covering the plot to replace the crossing guard at the school with a bucket of flags. Technology displacing the honest worker." Gerry paused, waiting for a reaction.

"What's next? Robots for teachers?" I asked, a weak attempt at humor.

Gerry stared at me in silence. Wit was his job, not mine. "Whatever. I handle the big stories." Gerry looked pleased with himself as he walked his chair over closer to me.

"We'll air this in the next day or two. Why don't I have you in every week over the next month, to build momentum? With my help, you might pull this off." The announcer reached out a moist hand to squeeze my wrist and held on. "We've been like ships passing in the night, Val. You left for the city about when I moved here. Now you're back, we should go out for a beer, make up for lost time." He leaned in. "Talk business."

I'd rather replace a zipper in a pair of jeans, I thought. "Sure. Maybe. When I'm not so busy," I said, extracting my arm from Gerry's grip, my watch catching on the heavy links of the gold-plated bracelet on his wrist. Pulling myself free, I stood up too quickly and knocked a chair, with a crash, onto the studio floor.

And I left.

But before I closed the door behind me, I turned and looked back. There he was, the "Voice of the Waves" himself, classic rock in the background, electrical cords tangled around his feet, a broken chair in his hands.

My mind snapped a picture. I'd remember this.

CHAPTER TWO

It wasn't far from CKGC to the store, so I walked. I thought best on my feet. Could I pull this off? If the co-op didn't work out, there was no next idea.

As I neared the gray-green framed building where our family had done business for generations, I heard honking in the sky. I looked up. There were the Canada geese, coming back after a long winter down south. I wondered if the smell of the salt reached as high as the clouds and if it had led them back too.

A movement caught my attention. An expensive dark car pulled out from one of the diagonal parking spaces in front of the store. I was close enough to see the out-of-province plates.

In a town as small as this one, I wondered who it could be. It was too early for tourists, and most come-from-aways shopped across the causeway in the town of Drummond, because it was bigger. There were rumors of plans to grow our business district to compete and even some talk of a dollar store in the vacant lot next to us, but I didn't believe them.

I liked Gasper's Cove the way it was. Safe and uneventful. It was an old town, built in the days when half the British Navy was built with Nova Scotia timber and skill. Those days had sailed away, but the idea of making everything we needed with our own hands persisted. The children here wore home-sewn clothes to school, and mittens were knit for them in threes, in case one got lost. Basements were lined with jars of apples, pears, lobster, and moose meat, because the winters, well, the winters were too long. Folks around here knew how to do things. They would work with me on the co-op. I knew they would.

At the store, I pushed open the big glass doors, and I looked for my dog, Toby. There he was, at his post on the old recliner near the tool aisle, ready to wag hello and goodbye to customers as they came and went. Sure, Walmart might have greeters, but here at Rankin's we had Toby, our most popular employee, and the reason I'd put a basket of "Who rescued who?" stickers on the counter beside the cash register.

Ahead, my cousin Rollie was behind the cash register. I was never sure if Rollie ever brushed his hair, or if he did and it just didn't make any difference. I had dark, almost black, wavy hair like my mother, but Rollie had inherited the Rankin Celtic genes and wild red hair, but none of the temper. Rollie was known in the family for his hard-to-rattle nature. My aunt loved to talk about the night the stove downstairs set fire to the house, and Rollie, only five at the time, had got them all up whispering, "We might want to go outside for a bit."

We were all brought up with these stories, and each, in our own way, saw ourselves, and each other, as legends. I was the one who always took apart her Christmas presents to see what I could make with the parts. "Nail it down," my mom would say, "or Valerie will use it for crafts." My cousin Darlene, on the other hand, was the born caregiver, the one who once kept a dead bird hidden in her closet, convinced she could nurse it back to health. I remember how happy she was when my uncle, who had found and buried the tiny corpse, told her it had flown away, now fully recovered. And when I was very young, during storms I would hear my dad say, "Lash yourself to the mast," and I used to think if that happens, I'll find Rollie—he's a mast. And he was, too, then and now: tall, substantial, and steady. So, no surprise, when I found myself alone in an empty nest in the city, I decided, like Rollie, to come home.

Rollie held us together. When his mom went off to Florida with Aunt Dot, she'd left the family store without a manager. As I remembered, there had been a fourteen-second conversation about hiring someone who was not a relative to run the business, but Rollie had announced he would come back and take over. We were shocked by his offer, but grateful. After all, Rollie would be leaving a secure government job as a staff psychologist at Drummond Correctional Institute to sell fishing gear and bird feed, but he insisted this was what he wanted to do.

He was doing his best, but I often wondered if he had underestimated the difficulty of transitioning from counseling to selling. Granted, he did an excellent job with "How can I help you?" but taking money made him uncomfortable. We all tried to help. Today, twelve-year-old Polly Peters, our drop-in assistant, was showing him how to use the debit machine, her French braids and aquiline nose a contrast to the chaos of my cousin's undisciplined hair and wild beard—almost a mirror of their gap in technical understanding. When I walked in, Rollie smiled. He was relieved at the interruption.

"How did the interview go?"

"Okay, I think. I got the word out. Have you ever been there? It's sort of a wood-grain, broom-closet version of CNN." I hesitated, searching for a diplomatic way to describe the radio host. "That Gerry's a character."

"Oh yes, 'Voice of the Waves.' Ambitions larger than his opportunities," Rollie said. "Not an easy combination to live with peacefully."

"No kidding. But at least he offered to get me on the radio again. That will help. The pressure's on now," I said. "Which reminds me. How's the space coming along?"

"I've got Duck upstairs now," Rollie said. "Go have a look. He's working on the floor. There was spilled boat oil all over the place. Hardened into a real mess."

I headed toward the stairs, then stopped. I had a question. "Who did I see leaving in the fancy car just now?"

"Nobody. Nothing." Rollie did an imitation of someone unconcerned. "Some guy from Ontario."

Behind his back, Polly rolled her eyes. "That's not true. It wasn't nothing. He wants to buy the store."

I faced Rollie. "What are you talking about?"

Rollie studied the pressed metal ceiling above us. "It looks like they want the lot between us and the car dealership for a discount place. But there's a problem: no space for parking. Nobody's going to park on the water."

"Go on," Polly urged. "Tell her what he said about tearing this place down."

Rollie waved his hands back and forth in front of his face. "Don't make a big thing about this. It's not going to happen. Not ever. Over my dead body. I said no. The man left. End of story."

Polly was unconvinced. "Guy was a jerk. Asked me whose little girl I was. Told him I was here as an intern." She looked at Rollie for confirmation, and he shrugged.

Intern. Not a bad description for her, I thought. Last fall Polly had started visiting the store every school lunch hour rather than spend the time at her parents' real estate business down the street. She was a speedy eater and usually made short work of the pretzels and hummus her mother sent and kept herself busy before she had to go back to school by attacking new merchandise with the pricing gun, and dealing with difficult customers on the phone.

Satisfied with her new job description, Polly continued. "Toby didn't like that developer man either. Barked when he came in. He's never done that before."

This was true; Toby loved everyone. "Well, he's gone now," I said. "No one around here would shop in a chain store." I wasn't sure this was true, but it seemed like the kindest thing to say. "Why don't we go see what Duck's doing? Sooner we get more traffic in here, the better."

Donald "Duck" MacDonald arrived in Gasper's Cove shortly after Rollie returned. We assumed Duck was one of Rollie's former clients from the prison and was on some sort of parole/work/rehabilitation program Rollie had invented but never discussed. All we knew for sure was that my cousin trusted Duck. As a result, we figured if Duck had ended up in jail, it had to be because of his crazy brothers, all of whom were still incarcerated, for their own good and the good of the rest of Nova Scotia. The consensus was that if Duck hadn't been completely innocent, he probably hadn't been completely guilty either.

Tall, dark, and good-looking in an Elvis-Presley-before-Vegas sort of way, Duck spent his days doing anything Rollie wanted. Most of the time, this meant sweeping the floors and hauling in boxes of stock, but more recently, it had included converting the upstairs storeroom into a cooperative center for the arts. So far, Duck had managed to clean up generations of Rankin debris and was now replacing the sticky, broken floorboards.

It was a job Rollie believed he should supervise. Like many men who weren't practical themselves, Rollie loved to watch others work and give them the full benefit of his non-experience.

"No wonder the floor bowed. Look at those beams," Rollie said, down on his hands and knees over an open area where the boards had been lifted, exposing the structure underneath.

"Joists. Big one down the middle's the beam," Duck corrected. "Sure is a mess. Clean her out, cover her up. Good as new."

I moved in closer to look; I was sure I knew as much about this as Rollie. "Yuck! Is that what I think it is?" I asked. The smell was unpleasant but regrettably familiar.

"I'm afraid so," Rollie said. "Over a century of mouse poop and nests ... hey, watch the cat."

At the word "cat," Duck's head swiveled around, and he made a fast grab for Shadow, the current store cat, already halfway into a dark passage between the joists. "Come here, my kitten. Don't want you to get stuck," Duck cooed, scooping up the rangy gray cat, another rescue like himself, and holding her close. "Going to take you downstairs and put you in the office, until Daddy's done. Can't let you get hurt; kitten's gotta stay safe." The cat, who never, ever, ever let anyone hold her, looked up at Duck and nuzzled his neck. Entwined in deep communion, the two descended to the main floor.

Still squatted down over the ripped floor, I looked up at Rollie. "Do you think we can do this in time?"

"Of course we can," Rollie said. I noticed he had switched from his normal voice to his professional counselor soothing voice, the one which I usually found a little annoying but needed to hear today. I studied my cousin's face. I was sure that when Rollie worked as a therapist his kindness was his greatest attribute. I wondered if sitting with a good person, even if you weren't always sure you were one yourself, made a difference. I certainly hoped so.

But what did it feel like to provide that to people? "Do you ever miss it?" I asked. "You know, being a psychologist? What made you decide to leave? I mean, to come here and sell rakes and rope and try to figure out the debit machine?"

Rollie was silent as he slowly dusted the sawdust off his khaki pants. "It wasn't the work; it was visiting day. The empty chairs." He looked up and saw the puzzled look on my face. "Most of the inmates didn't have anyone come and see them. Mothers, or someone wanting money, but that was it."

"That's sad, but how was it your problem?" I asked. "Weren't you there to get those guys in better shape for the outside world, so they could fit in?"

"I used to think that was my job," said Rollie, "but after a while, it became clear to me I was at the wrong end of the business. Those men weren't abandoned because they committed crimes; they'd committed crimes because they were abandoned."

"Ah, that makes so much sense," I said, suddenly proud of my cousin. Just because someone looked disorganized on the outside didn't mean the inside of their head couldn't have everything lined up right. Rollie was proof of that.

"This," my cousin said, tapping his foot on a pile of old floorboards, "is where the real work is. It's what we inherited." He paused and looked over my shoulder as if he could see someone I couldn't. "During the war, you know how many men left their wills with Grandpa? Fifteen. In a town this size." He pointed to the front of the building. "Our name is out front. Rankin. I couldn't be the one to break the chain."

"I understand. I really do," I said. I was a Rankin too.

"Only one problem." Rollie's large pale blue eyes were wistful. "I have no idea how to run a store myself, how to do this. None at all."

I opened my mouth to say something wise and supportive, but before I could, Polly's voice rose through the stairs.

"Rollie, better come down here, quick," she called, her young voice shrill, urgent, and concerned. "There's someone here to see you. From the town offices. A building inspector. You've been reported."

CHAPTER THREE

Kenny MacQuarrie from the town council offices stood at the bottom of the stairs. Toby and I often passed Kenny and his elderly bulldog on our walks. Sometimes I wondered if my dog and I would end up looking the same. Kenny and Max certainly did—they were both squat, determined, slightly belligerent, and inclined to drool. I first noticed Kenny because he always carried spare plastic bags to pick up after any dog with less responsible owners, and often lent me some. Today, he was dog-less, bagless, and on the job, clipboard in one hand, a metal measuring tape in the other, and a flip phone clipped to his belt. This wasn't a social call. That was clear.

"All right, Rollie," Kenny called out as we hurried down the narrow stairs to meet him, indignation sharp in his voice. "Forget your building permit?"

"I didn't think I needed one for a small job like this," Rollie protested. "Nobody could see it."

Kenny sighed and gave the wall a look as if hoping to find support and common sense there. "Here's the thing—somebody did." To make his point, Kenny pushed past Rollie to climb to the scene of the illicit renovation, his nylon windbreaker rustling with official importance as he moved. Rollie and I made eye contact and followed. At the top of the landing, Kenny stopped, caught his breath, and looked around.

He had to be impressed. It was beautiful up here, with a large semicircular window and a panoramic view of the water completely wasted on a stockroom. Surely, even a building inspector would understand what a beautiful retail space this would become.

But Kenny couldn't see the future. "So, this was a storage area, right?" he asked, sniffing the air, no doubt picking up the scent of a nation of mice.

Rollie nodded. Kenny went quiet, walked over to where Duck had pried up the boards, and leaned over for a better look. My pocket buzzed. I hesitated. We had company, but I stole a look at my phone. A text. Two texts, three, four.

> Saw your sign. Knit a ton of mitts when I sat with dad at the hospital. Want them?

> I make whirligigs, those spinning lawn decorations. You know my place on the Shore Road. A garage full.

> Lobster rope wreaths. Guy told me you're selling stuff. Also bowls, doormats. Weatherproof. How much you think I could get?

> Anyone else doing quilted table runners? We should talk.

Another beep. It was Darlene, my best friend and a cousin who felt like a sister.

Lunch? New man. Tomorrow? 12:30? Agapi?

I rolled my eyes. Darlene and a new boyfriend? We'd barely finished workshopping the departure of chronically unemployed husband number three. She hadn't mentioned any of this when we talked two days ago. I hoped she hadn't found another shifty character she believed only she understood.

Kenny's metal tape snapped. I looked up. I could handle all this later.

"Okay. Rough lumber—that's what's been used. For keeping odds and ends up here, it's fine, but if you're going to have a crowd moving around, that'd be a different thing entirely." Kenny shook his head, amazed at the things people tried when he wasn't looking. "Like those decks. Perfectly safe for a bit of a BBQ, but then someone has a party, 30 people get on it, and the whole thing falls off the house. All about load. So, before you even think about opening this up, you'll need an engineer's drawing showing the spans. That will tell me if you need a new beam, which I think you do. And get a proper permit. I shouldn't have to say that."

"An engineer?" Rollie sounded unsettled.

"Yup," Kenny said. "You need drawings stamped by a professional engineer." He smirked, pleased with what he would say next. "Until we have those drawings, we're going to have to put a stop work order on this renovation. You can keep doing business in the rest of the store, but what you're doing up here, it's got to be put on hold."

15

"Geez, Kenny, do you have to?" Rollie asked. "Valerie's put out the call. We need to get this space ready for those Tourism folks from Halifax. You can imagine what they're like, and we've only got a few weeks."

"Not my problem." Kenny shot a look at me. "This situation is bigger than any person's pet project. Safety issue. I have no choice. Got to shut her down."

∽

Once Kenny left, Rollie and I walked silently down the stairs, each of us trying to absorb what had just happened. Looking out from the dim interior of the old store to the bright sunlight of the street outside, I saw Kenny march off to a car with a magnetic "Building Inspection—Eastern District" sign stuck to the side. I watched him take out his keys and move to unlock the driver's door, then stop, his eye caught by something on the boardwalk. Moving quickly, he ran off to pursue a discarded chip bag as its open mouth caught the spring breeze and lifted it into the air. Silently cheering for the bag, I held my breath as I saw Kenny swoop up and catch the thin plastic just before it sailed away to litter the water in the bay. Satisfied, he crumpled the bag into a tight ball, stuffed it into the zippered pocket of his windbreaker, and returned to the car to drive off, indicating before he turned at the end of the empty street.

Rollie came up beside me and put a large hand on my shoulder. "Come on now, Val. Let's go to the office, have a cup of tea, and talk this through. No need to panic."

"Speak for yourself," I said, following my cousin into the small room by the back door, the place where Rollie pretended to do accounts and, more often, listened to locals needing someone to talk to.

As soon as we had closed the office door behind us, I lifted Shadow out of the well-worn visitor's chair and sat. Moving to the tiny counter above an ancient bar fridge, Rollie slowly and deliberately made us tea—chamomile for me and black tea with milk and two sugars for himself.

I waited. Rollie always liked to think before he spoke. I wondered what that felt like.

"I know an engineer over in Drummond, a good guy. I'll call him," Rollie finally said. "We can't get too worked up yet; we need to get the facts first. I feel responsible. I had no idea we couldn't use the space up there."

"It's not your fault; it's mine," I said. "If I hadn't started this, no way Kenny would have come out, and no way anybody would be talking to engineers. The store was fine the way it was." I felt a chill. "We don't have money for a new beam, do we?"

Rollie picked up a spoon and slowly stirred another sugar into his mug. "There's not much left on the store's line of credit, to be honest. I hoped something new, like this tourism thing, would help us work it down. You had a good idea; it's still a good idea. Don't blame yourself. What do we know about beams? And what did Kenny call it? Loads?"

He was right, but before I could say anything, there was a knock at the door. Duck stuck his head in. "There's a couple of people out here who want to leave stuff for Val. One lady's got a box of beeswax candles, and there's a guy with a bunch of beach rock birds. Where do you want me to put it?"

"Take it all out back," Rollie said. "We'll be there in a bit."

Duck shook his head; these new crafty arrivals would mess up his system for stacking bags of peat moss and lawn seed in the limited space at the rear of the store. To make the point, he sighed as he eased the door closed.

Alone again, I turned to Rollie. "Listen. You contact this engineer because you know him, but I want to be the one to deal with this, understand? My project, my responsibility. I want to do this by myself." I calculated my credit card cash advances in my head. How much were engineers? Did they take installments?

"You don't need to do that. It's not necessary," Rollie said, as I expected he would.

"Of course it is." I paused. "You've been great, letting me start classes here at the store. Just like Aunt Dot gave me her house to sit after she and your mom went to Florida. But I need to do something just myself. I left the city to come back here for a reason." I took a sip; the tea was hot. How did I explain this to someone who had only had real jobs, who had always had security? "I've never done work or had a project that was only mine. I was always just trying to make ends meet—take care of myself and the kids. I have a box of plastic name tags in the back of the closet, from my jobs. Why did I keep them? I don't want any more. I want to make something no one can take away from me in a place I don't have to leave."

Rollie stared into his mug and then at me. "Okay, I can see how you need this. But promise me that you will let me help where I can."

"I will. Don't worry."

"Good. That's settled." Rollie hesitated, looking at the bills, invoices, and unopened envelopes scattered all over his desk. "But there's something else that's bothering me. How did we get here? Who reported us? Why would anyone in town stir this up?"

⌒○⌒

Later, when Toby and I were home and in bed, I thought about Rollie's question. Next to me, the dog was asleep, his universe contained in this moment—no memories behind him, no worries ahead—but even his solid form and loud, deep breathing couldn't keep my cousin's words from whirling around in my head. Who cared what went on in the second story of an old store? Had the mysterious developer, the one who wanted to replace our building and history with parking spaces, called in Kenny?

I had to know.

At three a.m., I remembered Julie Chandler. Julie and I had worked together once at the mall, stocking shelves before Christmas, and we'd kept in touch. When the season ended, I moved on. Julie found something at the property management office and had done well.

I got up and grabbed my laptop.

Hi, Julie. It's been a while, but I have a favor to ask. Are you able to get info on an out-of-province developer for me? Someone working with the dollar stores and interested in a lot on Front Street in Gasper's Cove? They might be after the family property. Any help appreciated. Next time I'm back in the city, we'll get together. Take care. And thanks, Valerie.

I went back to the bedroom. While I'd been up, Toby had moved over to sprawl across the pillows on my side of the bed. With effort, I heaved him over and slid my body into the narrow strip he left me, and got under the covers. I couldn't sleep. Usually, taking action was all I needed to settle myself down, but not tonight. Instead, I lay in the dark and listened to the wind stirring up the tops of the trees. The room dimmed as the clouds moved over the moon's face, turning that light out. Disturbed and awake, I thought about the town outside the house, traveling in my mind to the dark yard out back, down the long street, down the hill, to the black water in the bay. I thought about the hills behind us, and the rutted muddy tracks in the woods. Anyone, or anything, could be up there, and only the animals would see it as they stepped back into the shadows of the bushes. It was a crazy thought, a middle-of-the-night-alone thought, but I suddenly had a sense of something without good intentions moving toward the community. I knew I was being foolish, but I felt something out there, so strongly I could almost see it, and then wondered if it saw me too.

CHAPTER FOUR

I drifted off around dawn. I was finally getting some sleep when the front doorbell buzzed. Groggy and with the mood of the night still with me like the remnants of a bad, half-remembered dream, I struggled to focus. I wasn't ready for visitors, but I rushed down the hall in my slippers and purple velour housecoat anyway. This was probably Darlene with news or gossip that couldn't wait until lunch. That would be it.

Pulling the door open, I was surprised to see a young man, not much older than my sons, on my front steps. I didn't recognize the face—pale, thin, and sharp, with bright eyes behind round glasses—but his earnestness was familiar.

"Sorry to bother you. I'm Noah Dixon, you know, from the radio station."

"Yes, you work with Gerry," I said, pulling my housecoat tighter around my neck. "What can I do for you?"

"You haven't heard? Of course not—it's early."

"Heard what?" Last night's uneasiness returned.

"It's Gerry. He's dead. The police were there when I got to work. Someone from the credit union found him at the bottom of the stairs."

Those steep, slippery, carpeted stairs. I'd climbed them myself just yesterday. They were an accident waiting to happen. The poor kid. But why was he at my door?

"That's awful. Listen—would you like to come in?" I asked. Noah wasn't much older than my son Paul, at school in New York, so far away.

"That would be nice, thank you." Someone had raised this boy well. "I would like to talk to you. It looks like you were his last interview. I've got some questions."

"Sure," I said, opening the door wide, blocking Toby with my foot to keep him from knocking my visitor over. "Don't mind the dog. He's friendly." I made room for Noah's jacket in the small coat closet. "Had breakfast? I think we need a coffee."

Once we'd settled at the kitchen table, I sat and sipped from my mug, watching Noah eat. I'd put cheese and a banana on the plate with his toast. All the food groups.

"How long have you worked at the radio station?" I asked.

Noah wiped his mouth with a piece of paper towel.

"Just a few months. I'm doing journalism. This was my last work term. I know Gerry seemed like a loser, but he was teaching me a lot. He used to joke, 'You and me are like Woodward and Bernstein, kid, and I'm the good-looking one.'" He swallowed hard and went quiet. "He was always trying to find some scandal to blow open."

"In this town?" I asked, remembering the bluster of the man in the pilled vest.

"I think Gerry was onto something this time." Noah was defensive. "I wonder if he said anything to you."

"Like what? We talked about my plans for selling local crafts. That's all," I said, interested, despite myself.

"I asked him a couple of days ago what he was working on, but he wouldn't tell me. Said it was too early. He was waiting for something from the library." The young reporter looked wistful. Gerry would be missed. "He'd only say one thing: 'No one knows what evil lurks in the mind of jerks.' Classic Gerry."

Gerry, I suspected, knew a few things about the minds of jerks. "Maybe you'll never find out what he meant," I said. "It sounds like he had a bad accident. That's something that could happen to anybody."

"I guess." Noah didn't sound convinced. "The police said the same thing—that it looked like he fell and hit his head. They asked me about drinking and drugs." He swallowed. "Beer, sure, but Gerry was too cheap for drugs. And there's something that bothers me."

"What's that?"

Noah dug out his phone and handed it to me. There was a missed call from CKGC late last night. "The RCMP officer I talked to, Corkum, said it was probably a pocket dial when he fell. I'm not so sure."

"Why not?"

"There was no reason for Gerry to be at the station that time of day. I think he wanted to talk." He stopped to sip his coffee. "They're going to do an autopsy."

"Wouldn't that be normal? They know what they're doing."

"Do they? Look—I'm a reporter. He was bashed up pretty bad, facedown at the bottom of the stairs." Noah's voice shook. Then he lifted his face, defiant. "It was no accident."

"Are you telling me you think someone murdered Gerry?" I asked, looking around the kitchen at all the pairs of my aunt's extensive salt and pepper shaker collection. I'm sure this was the first time they'd heard a conversation like this.

"That's exactly what I am saying. Murder. It's why I'm here," said Noah. "If you can remember anything—anything—it would help. I've got to do this."

"Do what?"

"I need to find out. Who's the jerk?"

CHAPTER FIVE

After Noah left, I poured myself another cup of coffee and sat. I didn't know what to think. My first reaction was that this couldn't be happening. Not here in a town like this. Nothing terrible ever happened in Gasper's Cove. That was the point. That was why I'd come home. Surely the police would handle it. There was nothing I could do, or should do. I wondered where Noah's mother was. Did she know how her son was feeling today? What challenges did my kids have that I didn't know about? I hoped if they needed to talk, someone was there.

Murder. If Noah was right, the police would confirm it. I had a sudden, uneasy thought. If someone had killed Gerry, they'd come sometime after I left. What if I had stayed longer?

Toby and I were late for work. It was a beautiful spring Nova Scotia day—the air clean, salty, and sharp—so I decided to walk down to the waterfront and the store rather than drive. However, whatever plans I had for early morning exercise were completely lost on Toby, who managed to take three meandering steps backward to every one of my steps forward, as he sniffed the smells recently released by the melted snow. When we finally arrived, Rollie took one look at me and knew I needed to talk.

"I heard about Gerry," he began. "An awful thing. I knew his voice more than the man himself, but still, someone you know. Are you okay?"

"I can't believe it, to tell you the truth. I feel stunned." I pushed Toby over on the recliner and sat down. "Plus, there's something else," I said, stroking Toby's large silky head to steady myself. "Gerry's assistant, understudy, or whatever you call him, came to see me. He doesn't think Gerry's death was an accident." To my surprise, Rollie didn't dismiss the idea.

"Murders happen," he said. "More often than you think. I learned that in my last job. And I met more than a few killers at the prison. You'd be amazed at how ordinary they were."

"Really?"

"Absolutely. Everybody has a breaking point. Most of us never get anywhere near ours. Killers are different. They get there faster. I don't think random killings happen often. Something sets them off." Rollie's eyes moved to the rows of tools, but his mind was somewhere else, remembering. "I knew a guy once who killed a neighbor who left the porch light on all night. It shined into this guy's window and kept him awake. So, one evening, he went over and smashed in the light, then his neighbor's skull. Most of us would have bought a window blind."

"That's nuts. So, every murder has a motive—you just need to find it? See things the way the murderer does?"

"I'd say it helps. There are two things about killers, although I'm not sure if this applies to Gerry. That's for the police, not us, to decide. But here it is. It seems to me there is always a motive, even a crazy one. The second thing is a killer nearly always gets caught. Someone eventually figures it all out. No murderer I've ever met was half as smart as he thought he was. And they all believed they were pretty smart."

I thought this over. Noah might be right, but why would anyone want to kill Gerry? His dress sense? His breath? He was a reporter. Had Gerry been killed to keep something from going public? How would we ever know what that was, or who would kill to keep it hidden, now that the announcer was gone? It was overwhelming.

"Val, don't get yourself too tied up in this kid's theory." My face was easy to read, and Rollie had read it. "Leave this up to the authorities. You and I have other business to take care of this morning. Remember my engineer friend? He did me a favor and came by last night, then went home and wrote up a report. He's not going to charge us, but one of us needs to go over and hear what he has to say."

"I'll go. I said I wanted to handle it. And besides, I need an outing."

"I think you do. My friend said he'll be in all day, so just drop by. You'll like him. Here's the address, over in Drummond," Rollie handed me a business card, and then took Toby's leash. "You stay with me, big guy. We'll have a good time." The dog slapped his tail back and forth and beamed at Rollie, a human he understood.

I grabbed my purse and left them, relieved to have a job to do, something different. I walked back to my house and jumped in my car. As I drove, I felt myself relax. I turned on the radio. After the weather report—cloudy with a chance of sun, or maybe sunny with a chance of showers—my interview, and Noah, came on.

"Good morning, listeners. As many of you know, the unexpected death in the news was our own Gerry Richards. In his memory, I am going to play his last segment. There was only one 'Voice of the Waves.'"

Our interview came on, and it was then I realized the power of radio. There was no hint of the tired and worn space we'd sat in, or of two slightly desperate middle-aged people trying to make something of themselves. No one listening could hear that. Only our voices existed.

I was surprised to hear myself, voice high, words rushed. I sounded like an amateur, and I was, but Gerry sounded like a pro. The sound of his rich baritone filled my car, and I felt a deep, sudden sadness. You'd never know to look at him, but Gerry knew what he was doing. I had underestimated the man. I let my mind wander. What if someone else had made the same mistake, and then decided the only way to silence Gerry was to murder him?

The interview ended.

I was almost there. The office was on Adelaide Street, not hard to find, in downtown Drummond, the larger town on the mainland connected by a causeway to Gasper's Island and our community of Gasper's Cove. What would Stuart Campbell, the engineer, say about the stop work order on the renovations? Would I understand everything in his report? Numbers always made me nervous. I hoped it wouldn't show.

The office of S.J. Campbell, Engineering Limited, was above the Peking Palace restaurant, where the kids and I had eaten the last time they'd visited. Campbell was at the back of the building, between Dr. Peter Naugler, dentist, and A-1 Tax Specialists. The scent of garlic and black bean sauce rose all the way up to their floor. As I climbed the stairs, I wondered how anyone could work here and not be hungry all the time.

The hallway at the top of the stairs was quiet, but the engineer's door was slightly ajar. I went in, entering a small empty reception room with four vinyl chairs and a low table covered with ragged copies of *Atlantic Boating* and last week's newspaper. Topographical maps of the coastline were framed and hung on the wall, along with a puzzle of an old schooner, carefully assembled and mounted behind glass.

I hesitated.

This was a smaller operation than I'd expected. There was no receptionist to tell me what to do next, and no bell to ring, so I sat. Through the smoked glass door to the inner office, I heard a male voice talking. Rollie had called ahead, and Campbell was expecting me, but the longer I waited, the more nervous I felt.

I remembered my phone and pulled it out to turn the ringer off. I had a new message and a picture of something that looked like large chopsticks. I knew what they were.

Spurtles for stirring oatmeal. Tourists love them.
Can make as many as you want. Assorted woods.

Very nice …

I started to reply but before I could press *send*, a door opened, and someone said my name. I looked up.

Stuart Campbell was about my age; it is hard to tell with men. He had on construction boots and jeans, and an open-neck dress shirt, well pressed, probably at the cleaners, with the sleeves rolled up. I noticed a large, heavy black watch covered in dials and a yellow band against cancer on his wrist. His hair was curly and dark, though not as dark as mine, and his eyes were a very bright blue. I detected a small hole in one earlobe from a long-removed earring and no wedding ring.

"Valerie Rankin?" he asked and looked around, so as not to confuse me with all the invisible people packed in the waiting room.

"That would be me." I stood and followed the engineer into the office.

"Here—have a seat," Stuart said, dusting off the nicest chair in the room. There were framed degrees on the wall and a good view over the water to Gasper's Cove. "Sorry about the mess. I've been doing some filing."

Looking at the piles of folders and papers on the floor beside the desk, I doubted if much filing was being done, but I let it pass. I wanted this man to tell me what I wanted to hear, so we could get back to renovating the co-op space at the store. I didn't have time to waste.

Stuart settled himself behind his desk and pulled a folder and a large roll of drawings toward him. "Nice day out there, isn't it?" he asked. "Good to see the snow finally go."

I wasn't feeling in the mood for small talk. I'd feel better when we got down to business. "So, Rollie told you about our

30

visit from the town?" I asked, ignoring any discussion of the weather. "Kenny has shut down our renovations. I'm here to see what we do next."

Stuart considered me calmly. He wasn't going to let me rush him.

"Yes. Kenny. The man with the rules. I talked to Rollie about that visit. We curl together, you know? Great guy. Always got time for Rollie."

More time than I have for you, I thought. *Let's get to the point.*

Catching my impatience, Stuart opened his folder. "I went out and saw the issue Kenny picked up on." He turned around a series of pictures on the desk so I could see them. "You see this a lot in older buildings. We ran into a similar situation with Chatham House down the street. Like this. An old beam was cut into years ago for the heating system. When they did that, they weakened its integrity. See—that's what's happened here in your place." He used his pen to show me cutouts in the wood. There were a lot of them.

"So, what does that mean?" I asked. "Is this why we got the stop work order?"

Stuart nodded. "Yes and no. It means the beam's fine for the way the store is running now, but it isn't strong enough to accommodate more traffic on the second floor. Kenny's right. It's not up to code for increased load. It has to be fixed before you can use the space for your craft retail idea."

Even I could figure out beams were big and replacing them would involve more money than either Rollie or I had. "So what do we do? What's going to happen next? I have a hard deadline. They are coming up to do a shoot for the tourism guide." I'd told the people at Tourism that the crafters' co-op was at the grand opening stage, not at the stop work order stage. "We need to get onto the website this year if we're going to have any chance at all this season."

Stuart nodded sympathetically. "I get it, but the old wooden beam needs to be taken out and a steel beam put in before you can open to the public. Pretty straightforward. They do it all the time. Shouldn't take more than a day."

"We only have a month, little more."

"Then you'll have to get on it, I guess."

"No kidding, but this all sounds expensive." I had no budget for my scheme. It was the second floor of Rankin's General or nothing.

Stuart wasn't finished. He hesitated, then pulled out another series of photos, again arranging them carefully in front of me.

"There's a secondary problem, and it's more serious," he said. "That old beam has been weakened and is sagging, probably has been for years. Over time, it's opened a crack in the walls." He pointed to a picture taken from outside the building. There was a dark fissure visible under the shingles, and he tapped it with his pen.

"I can see what you mean," I said, wishing I couldn't.

"The crack's let in the water. Now, you've got rot and a real mold problem. You'll have to deal with it soon. It's all in my report. Kenny's got his copy; this one's for you," he said, handing me a large brown envelope.

This was worse than I had expected. "Let's make sure I understand this," I said. "First, there's a beam that's got to be replaced right away before I can do anything upstairs. Next, the store's going to fall apart if we don't fix this," I added, gesturing to the mold and rot pictures. "Am I right?"

"I wouldn't put it exactly that way. But, more or less, that's it."

The back of my neck hurt. "How much?" I asked.

Stuart gathered up the photos. "You'll need a contractor to give you an exact quote. But I know Rollie. I can give you some sort of ballpark, just for the beam, right now." He tore a corner off a page on his desk, wrote some numbers, and pushed the scrap of paper over to me.

He watched me read. A lot of zeros. Way too many.

I raised my eyes. There was compassion on Stuart's face. This annoyed me more than anything he'd said. I was sure he thought I was a naive woman with big ideas and nothing to back them up with. I sat up straight.

"Thank you for your time," I said and stood. The handle of my purse caught on the chair. I struggled to get it free and then stumbled. Trying my best, I pulled my dignity around me like a coat and walked out, leaving behind me this man with his professional opinion, his secure job, his pressed shirt, and his non alphabetized files. Out I went, through the empty waiting room with its day-old paper, down the linoleum staircase, and into the street, the breeze, and the slap of the cool ocean air.

What would I say to Rollie?

CHAPTER SIX

I knew I couldn't drive until I calmed down, so I went to the car, tossed Stuart's brown envelope onto the back seat, and went for a walk.

Who had days like this? First, there was a story of murder over breakfast, and then, news of a disintegrating family business before lunch. Here I was, the person who had wanted to come back and lead a quiet life. What disruptive force had followed me here from the city? This wasn't the Gasper's Cove I remembered.

As I walked, I felt uneasy, as if someone was behind me. I looked back. No one, only the faces of small office buildings, corner stores, and restaurants, mixed in with old houses taken over by professional offices. Among those, I counted two dentists, an orthodontist, an insurance broker, a dermatologist, a florist, and four law firms. If I was being watched, it was from behind louvered blinds or heavy, expensive curtains.

I stopped walking. I was in front of Chatham House, the building Stuart had mentioned. The gray-shingled walls stared back down at me, waiting. *So, you had an undersized beam and a leaky wall too.* I spoke to it silently, moving close to look for signs of rot, mold, or deterioration. *Someone had the cash for repairs. Lucky you.* The house remained silent. I sighed and turned the corner. Then, almost missing it, I noticed the plaque on the side of the building:

Chatham House was the residence of Henry William Chatham 1772–1843, sea captain, out of Drummond, Nova Scotia. This house was occupied by Chatham and his descendants until its sale in 1978. The building is an outstanding example of the use of local materials by the region's master shipbuilders, reflecting many of the same construction details seen on the sailing ships built during that era. As such, it has been designated a protected historical property by the Province of Nova Scotia.

THE NOVA SCOTIA HERITAGE SOCIETY

I studied the plaque and read it again. Then I turned around and walked back the way I'd come.

The waiting room was still empty. I marched through it, up to the inner office I had just left, and knocked.

"Be with you in a minute," said the voice on the other side of the frosted glass. I heard the rustle of paper being crumpled and the sound of a paper cup hitting the edge of a wastepaper basket and rolling onto the floor.

The door opened. Stuart was surprised to see me. The room smelled of french fries and coffee.

"Forget something?" he asked.

"No." I walked past him and sat, my purse pressed protectively to my chest. "I have to ask you a question."

"Okay, what about?" Stuart asked as he sat down behind his desk.

"What can you tell me about heritage properties?"

"I'm not sure I follow." Stuart leaned back in his chair.

"Look. You told me Rankin's General is a mess." Stuart protested, but I kept going. "Not great news. So, I went for a walk to settle down before I tell Rollie. I know what he's going to say, and I don't want to hear it."

"Don't want to hear what?"

"I don't want him to have to tell me he doesn't have the money to do the work. I don't want him to feel he has no choice but to sell the store. That would break his heart. Break my heart. Besides, you know if he sells, they'll just pave it to put up a parking lot." My voice shook. "Like the stupid song."

The corners of Stuart's mouth moved, and then he went serious. "You are talking about the development proposal. Yes, I know about it. They're looking for more property." He studied me warily, as if assessing the chances I would go hysterical in his one good chair.

I wouldn't let that happen. I'd hold it together and get the information I needed. "Chatham House. Heritage site. Protected property. Tell me. How do we get that for us?" My voice sounded loud in the small room.

"I see. Interesting idea." Stuart thought it over. "The Heritage Property Act of Nova Scotia. Assuming that's what you mean. I'd have to look into it, but off the cuff, I'd say there's a good case the building has the history to be protected." He paused. "This is where this is going, right? You want the store to be designated so no one can tear it down?"

I smiled, and he smiled back. A nice smile.

"You got it. What does it take to make that happen?"

"Surprisingly, it's not complicated. The province makes the final call, but the real onus is on the town. All they have to do is make the argument that the structure is an important part of the built heritage of the community. It's up to them to apply."

Hope. A glimmer of hope. Something to hold on to.

That smile again. Stuart continued, "I have another thought. Assuming you get the designation, there are funds available to help in the remediation of historically significant buildings. I think that's what they did with Chatham House."

"Can you say that again? I want to make sure I get this right."

"Sure. If you can get Rankin's declared a heritage property, it's likely the province would pay for the renovations. A bank should give you bridge financing until the provincial money comes through. That's how it usually works."

"This is fantastic," I said. I needed this. So did Rollie, and all the Gasper's crafters. "What do I do next?"

Stuart turned in his chair to look past me out to the water. I wondered if he was thinking he'd said too much, too soon, to me. "Here's the thing. First, you need to get in front of the council to make your case." He spun his chair around.

"The next meeting is the day after tomorrow. I know who to call. I could get you on the agenda."

"You'd do that? Really?" This was nice of him. "Let me know." I wrote my cell number on one of Stuart's business cards and pushed it back to him. "And I have another request."

"Shoot."

I needed to be ready. I was going to face the seats of power. "This Heritage Property Act of Nova Scotia. Do you have a copy I can borrow for a few days?"

CHAPTER SEVEN

This time, when I left Stuart's office, I drove straight to the Agapi and my lunch with Darlene. We'd been eating there since high school and always ordered the souvlaki plate: lamb roasted on short skewers with garlic, onion, lemon juice, and strong Greek oregano. I suspected that George Kousolas, the owner's almost-middle-aged son, still had the same crush he'd developed on Darlene when we were in school together. She was always served first, and there were inevitably more olives in my cousin's salad than in mine. I wondered if Darlene had noticed. I hoped she had.

I placed our orders as soon as I sat down. I was desperate to know what Darlene knew about Gerry's death. She did the entire town's hair in her basement salon, and if there was information in circulation, she'd have it. I also wanted to tell her about Noah's theory, and my meeting with Stuart Campbell. I didn't expect she'd be interested in heritage buildings, but I knew she'd want to know more about Stuart. With Darlene, it was always about the guy.

She was late, but I didn't mind. Darlene's clients didn't want to give her up, even for lunch. When she finally arrived, Darlene wasn't alone. With her were three men, two of whom I recognized, and one with short, pale hair, whom I didn't. The tallest of the group was Brent Cameron of Cameron Motors, the logo prominent on the size L polo shirt he wore over his XL body. Brent's dad had spent a lifetime building the business his son now managed with all the confidence and cheerfulness of a man who had worked for nothing and inherited everything. I noted that his father's influence had also secured Brent a seat on the town council and that this was one face I'd have to convince at the town meeting. Close to Brent, but not as close as Darlene, strutted Harry Sutherland, formerly of the fishermen's union, and now also a councilor. The third man, the one I didn't recognize, was a sharp-looking character in a fitted suit, wearing aggressively large, round designer glasses and soft, black slip-on shoes. Whoever he was, this man was not a local.

As they walked toward me, I noticed Brent's hand on Darlene's back as he guided her to our table. Nodding to me, Brent, Harry, and the stranger moved on to a booth of their own at the back, further from the door.

"Sit," I said to Darlene, ignoring her companions. "What can you tell me about Gerry? What are people saying?"

Darlene arranged her cutlery carefully on the paper napkin. "Well, it's all anyone can talk about, as you can imagine. We're shocked. But the word is that if Wade's doing the investigation, they'll never figure it out."

I knew what she meant. Wade was Officer Wade Corkum, of the Royal Canadian Mounted Police, and we'd gone to high school with him. The Wade we knew was always the guy who put more work into building his body than developing his mind and was proud of it. These days, Wade was undoubtedly an honest cop, but likely one more confident than competent.

"What about the new officer he's got working for him, Dawn Nolan? I know her landlords and they say she's very sharp and nice, too."

Darlene snorted. "All reasons why Wade won't listen to her. I wish her luck." Her food arrived. Darlene moved her water glass to make room and beamed at George. I started to count her olives. "You saw Gerry, didn't you, the day he died?"

"I did. I had an interview about this crafters' co-op thing." I bent over to smell the garlic and lemon of Darlene's souvlaki, then leaned back while my plate was slid in front of me. Why would we ever eat anywhere else? "Weird thing—like I was just telling Rollie, his assistant reporter, Noah, dropped by the house and talked to me. He thinks Gerry might have been killed because he was onto something."

"Are you serious?" Darlene thought this over. "A guy like Gerry was probably into things we don't know about. He was no angel; a lot of people didn't like him."

"What do you mean?"

"Someone in the family, doesn't matter who, got into some trouble a while ago. Nobody's business—anyone can make a mistake. But Gerry got on to it and was going to make it public. It wasn't easy, but Brent shut him down and threatened to pull the dealership's ads. Mister big reporter backed off."

First I'd heard of this. "Why didn't you tell me about this before?"

"It happened a long time ago, while you were away. I promised to keep it to myself. The point is, I wasn't impressed with Gerry Richards. Wouldn't be one bit surprised if he had a few enemies."

I thought of Gerry in his tiny rundown studio, trying so hard to be something he wasn't. Maybe he'd tried too hard. However, the reference to Brent Cameron gave me an opening.

"So now you and Brent are an item?" I asked, trying to keep the worry out of my voice. My cousin always let men choose her; she never chose them. I'd done a bit of that myself, but with Darlene it was a cycle. I looked across the restaurant to where George was entertaining a table of senior ladies. She could do better; she deserved better.

Making an elaborate job of pulling the grilled chicken off the skewers, Darlene didn't respond. Finally, she looked up at me, only to try to change the subject. "You should come in and let me do your eyebrows. Ever think about wearing more eye makeup?" My lack of interest in makeup, apart from mascara and lipstick, had always frustrated Darlene. A natural redhead with long wavy hair, Darlene worked hard to cover her freckles with foundation and had worn eyeliner every day since we were fourteen. She'd even told me once that she never went to bed without blush just in case the house caught on fire in the night and some handsome fireman came to rescue her. Darlene was practical like that; she liked to be ready for anything.

"With one green eye and one brown one? Are you serious?" I asked, pointing to my eyes. It was due to some Rankin gene my mother said was associated with a 'touch of the fae,' a psychic sense she said ran in my dad's side of the family.

Strangers sometimes commented on my eyes; my family thought they made me special.

"We can work around it. I can show you."

"Don't try to distract me. It won't work. Back to Brent. Seriously?"

"Don't say it like that. We have a lot in common. You know I'm interested in local government."

This was news to me; I'd be surprised to hear Darlene even voted. She didn't like to take sides. "When did this start?"

"He came in for a trim, and we got to talking. You know how it is."

"I don't, but go on."

"We were chatting, and then he called me an influencer because I know everyone." Darlene had finished eating and got out a coral lipstick. "Brent has big plans. He asked me to help. He wondered if I could do some informal polling for him, maybe run a few ideas past my clients, and listen to what they thought. He needs me. There is no one else to do this for him. How could I say no?"

Easily, I thought, very easily.

"This could lead to something, you know, more than hair. He told me he needs a communications liaison, someone with political instincts." Darlene's two matched blue eyes were wide with awe. "He thinks I'm full of undeveloped potential."

I looked at her. I had to be careful not to hurt Darlene's feelings. This went back to junior high; Darlene would believe anything. What was Brent's angle?

I shifted on the red vinyl seat of our booth and thought of how to approach this. "So what are Brent's ideas? What are the big plans?"

Darlene leaned forward, the bodice of her paisley print wrap dress slipping dangerously close to the oil and vinegar of her Greek salad.

"It's hard for him," she whispered. Looking over her head at the back of the restaurant, I saw Brent with a toothpick in his mouth. He seemed to be holding up well. "Brent's an ideas guy. He and Harry are the progressive wing at the council. But it's not easy going up against the reactionary forces." A wing? Reactionary forces? In a council of five people?

Darlene saw the look on my face. "Brent and Harry have a vision for the future."

Had Darlene morphed into a speech writer behind my back? Why was this reminding me of a campaign speech?

She was on a roll. "But those other people on the council. Linda, the librarian? My uncle Frank? Nice people, but, excuse me for saying this, the only vision they have is of the past. And then there's the warden. Mack wouldn't know a vision if it fell out of the sky and hit him on the head." Darlene's voice rose; there was no stopping her now. "You can't look back to go forward." Darlene sat back, pleased with herself. I thought she sounded like a lawn sign or something she'd read on Pinterest.

I slumped in my seat, trying to think of a diplomatic response. "You do know, don't you, that I'm going to council the day after tomorrow to ask them to make the store a heritage property? Get them to preserve it? You know, the past?"

Darlene gave me a long look. "Yes, I heard something, so here's my advice. Before the baklava arrives, why don't you go talk to Brent and Harry now? Warm them up for the meeting?"

This wasn't what I wanted to do, but she was right. I had to start somewhere, so I got up and walked to the back booth. There were three Western sandwiches on that table. At the best Greek restaurant in the region. This said it all.

"Gentlemen, can I have a word?" The three men stopped talking and looked at me without smiling. I was interrupting something serious.

Brent wiped the ketchup off his mouth. "Of course. Have a seat. Always time for an old friend. Let me introduce Lars Nyberg."

Nyberg? Was this stranger the guy who'd come to the store and tried to get Rollie to sell? I pulled up a chair from a table across the aisle and sat. No way I wanted to share a bench seat with this crew.

"I'm speaking at the council this week," I said. Brent and Harry nodded. "There's talk a developer wants our property for parking." I stared hard at Nyberg. He gave me a bland look back.

"Sure." Brent leaned back in his seat, further away from me. "As I understand it, Rankin's might be at the end of its life, structurally speaking."

"Yeah, like it's going to fall down," Harry added.

Of course, I realized, they'd heard about Kenny's visit.

"Not exactly falling down—far from it," I said, catching the "calm down," look in Darlene's eyes from across the room. "Our store's been here for generations. We need the council's support to protect it."

"Good luck with that." Harry grinned, looking to Brent and Nyberg for approval.

Brent ignored his fellow councilor, crumpled up his napkin into a ball, threw it down over the crusts on his plate, and pushed himself out of the booth to stand over me. "Time we headed out. Harry, Lars." He stared down at me, still seated. "Love to see citizen engagement," he said, and, good politician that he was, he reached out to pump my hand. I kept my hands in my lap.

"Yeah, nice to see interested parties, particularly the cute ones." Harry smirked at me as he moved past my chair to follow Brent and the man who had to be a developer out past the row of booths.

I watched the three walk toward the door. At our table, Brent leaned down and whispered in Darlene's ear. They both glanced over at me.

"See you at the meeting," Brent called out. "Looking forward to it."

"You should be," I called back. "Going to make history," I added, with no idea what that meant, none at all. Then I pulled out my phone and tapped out another email to Julie Chandler in Halifax.

Hi Julie. It's me again. I now have a name. Lars Nyberg. Any way you can check him out? I owe you. Something's up. Val.

CHAPTER EIGHT

After our lunch, Darlene left to do a house call on Mrs. Smith. "Fourteen hairs and every one of them permed, bless her." I stood on the sidewalk outside the restaurant. Brent and Harry had no time for me and my ideas; I hoped the other two councilors would be more supportive. Of those, I'd start with Linda, the town's long-standing librarian, and so by training likely to be more polite.

The library. Noah had mentioned Gerry wanted something from the library. What was it?

None of my business, but that didn't mean I wasn't going to find out.

It was a short walk.

The Gasper's Cove library occupied an old Dominion of Canada bank building one street up from the water. It had been built in the days when everyone believed the fish would jump into the boats forever, and its tall sandstone columns and an imperial portico reflected that long-gone optimism. I noticed that the date the bank was built was carved into the stone in Roman numerals, either 1923 or 1933 (it had been a long time since I was in school), alongside a pledge that this fine institution would "select its customers carefully, serve them well, and together duly prosper."

No longer a center of commerce, but now a location for book borrowing, toddler story-time reading, doing homework, and interest group meetings, the building was in the capable hands of head librarian and town councilperson Linda, library technician Catherine Walker, and an army of senior volunteers. The adult books were on the main floor, directly opposite the heavy brass-handled doors of the entry. Off to the side, books were checked out at what had once been a teller's window. The children's collection and a well-used toy lending library were on the floor below, in a cool and windowless dungeon painted in shiny red enamel, apparently to cheer the place up and to distract young minds from the ominous bulk of a huge, locked safe dominating one corner.

Today, Catherine was on duty at the main desk upstairs, looking like a timeless librarian from a movie—in a tweed skirt and white blouse, with a cardigan draped over her shoulders, a chain straddling her upper chest connecting the top button on one side to the buttonhole on the other. The small brown eyes behind her half-lenses were alert and suspicious.

"Coming in to pay your overdue fines?"

"Sure," I said, pulling my wallet out of my purse. Obviously, I had to get past the sentry before I could speak to the boss.

Catherine sighed and pulled up my file on her desktop computer. I always took out a large stack of books but read them at my own pace. As a result, I ran a chronic tab at the library, like a drinker at the bar. Shamelessly, as a lover of books if not of rules, I watched Catherine clear my record. Once more a responsible citizen, I asked her where I might find Linda.

She snorted. "She's in back with Frank in the boardroom, between the 700s and 800s. Not working—probably in there talking council business. We're busy in here today, too. We're getting ready for the 200th-anniversary exhibit. The warden's forcing us to focus on local sports heroes. He sent over a stack of his own high school yearbooks." She rolled her eyes. "The male ego has no limits."

I made sympathetic noises and, with that done, left her to find the boardroom, another memory of the building's banking past. There it was, behind a tall oak door tucked between Arts and Recreation, my favorite section, and Literature. I knocked and went in.

The room's two occupants were at a large table, Darlene's uncle Frank at one end, and Linda, his fellow council member, at the other. Frank saw me first and stiffened, his rimless glasses at the end of his long nose, his thin, somber face pale above the sweater vest some patient person had knitted for him on very small needles. Her back to the door, Linda turned around when she heard me, twisting her coral turtleneck inside her denim jumper and knocking the glasses hanging from a chain around her neck into a stack of bound regulations. They'd been deep in conversation and were surprised to see me.

"Excuse me," I said, hoping politeness would help me ease into the room. "I thought I'd have a word with you about the council meeting."

"Right. I saw the agenda." Linda lifted her glasses to have a better look at me. "We were discussing that man from the radio. Tragic."

Frank nodded solemnly, with the practiced sympathy of the pastor he once was. "The mind can scarcely comprehend. Death is always an event of profound meaning," he intoned, taking in a big breath, warming to his subject, settling in.

"I know. Terrible," I said, cutting Frank off, then feeling bad as soon as I did. How was it possible that this little man, more tightly wound than the fingering yarn in the regular rows of his brown vest, was of the same genetic pool as his niece, my cousin and best friend, Darlene, the undefeated updo champion, fourteen proms running, of the Eastern Shore Charity Hairstylist Challenge? Families, like life, have many mysteries.

I turned to the librarian. "Did you know him well? The announcer? The Gerry Richards I met didn't seem like a library kind of guy."

"You'd be surprised," Linda said. "He loved interlibrary loans. He used to ask me to help him file Freedom of Information requests too." She stopped as a memory moved across her eyes. "He'd been in to look at microfiche the day before he died and made a copy. I sent the original back to the archives today."

"Really?" This was what I was looking for. "Can you tell me what was on it?"

"Not policy, but I guess it doesn't matter now. I'll look at the records and let you know. But that's not why you're here," Linda said.

"No, it isn't," I said, although this was only partially true. "I wanted to speak to both of you, in fact, to discuss a heritage designation for the store. We need to protect it from development."

"Ah, a fine old building," Frank said, removing his glasses to polish them with a large worn cotton handkerchief, now animated by an audience. "It's part of the integral fabric of the community. We'd do well to be mindful of the contributions of our early mercantile ventures and the provisions necessary to support fishing, and before that, the shipbuilding industries—"

"The meeting tomorrow," interrupted Linda. "What do you want us to do?"

"Support my proposal."

"Count on it." Linda interlaced her hands in front of her on the table, like we used to do on our desks at school, and sat up. "We need growth. No one can live in a museum." She gave her fellow councilor a sharp look. "But growth has to be thoughtful. Mr. Slick from Cameron Motors and his yesman sidekick don't get it."

"Agreed. But the warden. Where does he stand?"

Linda laughed. "You'll get his support if it means he doesn't have to do anything," she said, surprising me with the level of bitterness in her voice. "Mack's got his empire the way he likes it: hands to shake, ribbons to cut, and lots of time to go out on his boat. It's unlikely he'll vote for anything that looks like change. Why would he?"

Frank agreed. "May I speak as someone experienced in the fine art of politics? Offer counsel?" I nodded; he was going to say it anyway. "Make sure you frame your presentation at the meeting so the warden will perceive your proposal as in support of the status quo, of which he is certainly a beneficiary."

"Exactly what I just said." Linda glared at her colleague, then at me. "If this development isn't Mack's idea, he won't go for it. You can't trust him, but you can count on that."

By the time I pushed my way out through the library's big doors, leaving almost half of Gasper's Cove's town council to their earnest labors in the old boardroom, I was worn right out. Political intrigue and death weren't a usual part of my day. I needed to reset myself back to normal, and that meant some stress-free sewing. I had two choices of where to do this. Closest was my classroom at the store, where I taught Thursday night sewing classes. There, I had a good cutting table, a gravity-fed iron, a serger, and a vintage Bernina that could sew through concrete. But working at the store meant I would have to talk to people. I'd had enough of that for one day.

So instead, after retrieving a bouncy Toby from the store, I decided to go home to the absolute quiet of my aunt's basement and her vintage Singer. I'd learned to sew on that machine, the kind an earlier generation of housewives had kept in a cabinet until hoisting it up to sew, an operation like raising the *Titanic*. Modern machines had far more features, but they were just machines. This sewing machine was different, a hand tool, an extension of myself. We'd known each other a long time; the old Singer would help me think.

Back in the house, Toby and I shared some cheese and grape jelly on crackers and then descended to our subterranean studio, the dog licking my fingers for crumbs as we went down the stairs. At the bottom, I wiped my hands on the apron I always wore to sew and turned on the flickering overhead lights. I walked over to my sewing table and pulled out my project. This week I was working on a linen vest to wear on my dog walks, the fabric hopefully adding some elegance to what was an otherwise entirely pragmatic garment. Dog walking required a lot of pockets. This vest had big ones, to stow the poop bags, my phone, and the leash I would unclip once Toby and I were in the woods.

The instructions made no sense, and after half an hour of frustration and trying to make pleats in the corners so the pockets would be expandable, I heard the doorbell buzz upstairs. Happy to put down my scissors, I ran up the stairs and opened the door.

Neil Ferguson and his wife, Tilly, from down the street were on my doorstep, both clutching plastic grocery bags.

"Heard you on the radio about the crafts with poor Gerry. Very sad," Tilly started. "We knew him in person, you know. He came out and interviewed us once."

Her husband cut in. "Interviewed me, you mean, Till. Gerry was really interested in what's been done in the town over the years. I was a trucker, you know. Me and Gerry had a great chat, and a few laughs over some things I'd seen."

Tilly stared at her husband, anticipated that he was about to start another story where he was the star, and intervened. "What you were talking about—selling crafts—got us thinking," she said, holding her bag open to me so I could see the delicate, patterned knitting inside. "Neil and I like to do a little something when we watch the TV. I thought it was worth showing you. To sell, maybe. I do baby sets, matinee jackets, hats, booties. Neil here carves."

On cue, Neil reached into his bag. He held out his gnarled hand, knuckles large from arthritis, fingers bent from a lifetime of work, to show me. In his palm were tiny fish and birds, sanded and painted, little mementos of his life.

"I do miniature lobster traps and lighthouses too," he explained. "If you want to see those one time, I can bring them around. Small ones are real nice on the mantel; big ones on the lawn, or next to the mailbox along the road. To scale, just like the real thing."

Tilly watched my face closely, her gray eyes large, bisected behind bifocals. She was taller than her husband and, I could see, used to letting him ramble and then advocating for them both. "I can knit up two baby sets a week once I get going. We like to keep busy. It's no trouble."

"Yup," Neil said, looking at his wife with pride. "Got to keep this one occupied, or she'll be up to no good."

Tilly pretended to be offended and then turned to me. It was time to do business. She waited.

I'd been making pockets; I wasn't ready for this. I reached into Tilly's bag and pulled out a tiny knitted cardigan, lace leaves fanning out around the neckline. Someone would save a sweater like this and pass it down. "I am sure we can sell these, no problem," I said, aware this was a promise to us both.

Tilly and Neil, whom I suspected were both on pensions and lived on not much else, made eye contact, relieved.

"You'll hear from me once we get going," I said, heavily aware of the two smiling faces on my front steps. "This is going to work out well."

Was that true? The co-op was my own dream, entirely dependent on the future of an unused area of the family store. It was something I had invented, just to see if I could support myself by making things, the only activity I'd ever really enjoyed. But it turned out I didn't own that dream. The crafts coming to me all had some other creative soul's hope attached, like a gift tag.

What had I started? What if I let everyone down?

CHAPTER NINE

The town council met in a strip mall on the edge of town, in a room at the back of the municipal offices, accessed from behind the counter for paying parking fines and property taxes.

As a center of municipal or town power, the venue wasn't very impressive, but then again, neither was the council. There were just five members: four district councilors and the warden. The tiny size of our local government was not unusual. Nova Scotia was a small province, just under a million people, with nearly half that population in the capital city, Halifax, or within the three other largish regional municipalities. The rest of the province was divided into 45 other small municipalities—some larger towns, like Drummond; some formed around smaller settlements, like Gasper's Cove; and some made up mostly of memories, but still officially on the map. At various points, scholars at the university tried to understand why such a small province was fragmented into so many fiercely independent and self-important governing bodies, and they usually ended up blaming the clan structure, this being New Scotland after all. Defeated by this history, the provincial government in Halifax handled the situation by keeping the important jobs of health, welfare, education, and infrastructure for itself and letting the rest of the province continue to operate in its pattern of little kingdoms within the kingdom, each responsible for the things that occupied the local residents most, namely potholes, snow clearing, putting up signs for the tourists (some of them still usefully in Gaelic, like in Cape Breton to the north), and, of course, the designation of protected buildings.

It was this last municipal power that interested me. At Stuart's suggestion, I had printed off copies of the application form for heritage property designation. Each councilor would be required to review a copy of the application and, if they were in support, sign and forward it to the warden for submission to the province. As I understood it, the applications were like ballots, cast for or against protecting the store. The province's role was to count the votes.

I shuffled into the meeting with the other visitors, sat on a metal folding chair, and looked around. It wasn't a hard room to read. On one side of a long oak table sat Brent and Harry, the progressive, pro-development team, in support of the construction of a dollar store on a rocky lot across from a fishing wharf. On the other side, arms crossed and ready for intellectual and rhetorical battle, were Linda and Frank, my supporters

At the head of the table sat Mack McRae, almost National Hockey League player, one-time contractor, and now the warden. I was sure Mack considered this his best job yet and, I suspected, saw it as an opportunity as much as a responsibility.

Mack's wife, Maureen, was there to provide administrative as well as spousal support. She wore a Chanel jacket and pearls and sat near the front, a pen and old-fashioned steno pad in her hands, poised to take minutes. Stuart, Kenny, and Noah, with a bulky recorder inherited from Gerry over his shoulder, sat with me at the back of the room. Just before the meeting started, Darlene arrived, in a navy blazer partially concealing a coral cocktail dress, and sat next to me.

"Why are you here?" I whispered to her.

"Observing the democratic process, and giving support," Darlene said. She smiled brightly and waved her manicured fingers at Brent, who acknowledged her as he carefully unbuttoned his tailored jacket. Next to him sat Harry, who was slumped near the head of the table, submerged in the buckling lapels and floating shoulder pads of a jacket custom fit for another, more substantial man.

The warden cleared his throat.

"Good evening, gentlemen, and charming ladies." Mack swept his eyes around the room, stopping only for a lingering look at Darlene before dragging his attention back to the rest of us. "Quite the game last night, eh? What about those Bruins?"

"The agenda," interrupted Linda. "Let's get to the agenda."

Mack looked at her and slowly and deliberately removed a pair of smudged drugstore reading glasses from the pocket of his navy sports coat and adjusted them on a Roman nose adrift in the fleshy wreckage of his once-classic profile. Glaring at Linda, he snapped the paper in his hands and read aloud.

First was a report on the work to be done to the water treatment plant, with a translation by Stuart. Next, there was a debate on whether a subcontractor and a friend of Mack's had overbilled on salting last winter's roads. Mack didn't think so. Following that, Frank gave a lengthy description of preparations for the 200th-anniversary exhibit at the library, during which most members got up and poured themselves a coffee. Finally, there was an extended discussion on increased funding for the summer's annual boat parade, and a vote—three for, two against.

"Just about does it," Mack announced, pleased to have once again diverted public funds to the maintenance of his sailboat. He was ready to go home. "Except for some miscellaneous business," he said, peering down at his paper. "What's this, Maureen? Something about the library and a heritage building?" He looked up at his wife.

"Minor business," she said, mouth tight, "if we have time."

"Time, if we keep it moving," Mack said. "Linda?"

"I want to discuss computers for the library. We need more public access." Linda began to distribute notes. "We have to think about the digital divide between rural and urban communities."

Harry snickered. She ignored him.

"Computers don't come cheap," said Mack. "And I have to wonder now if you are talking as a councilor or as a librarian. Where are we supposed to get that kind of money?"

"We could start by cutting back on the beers at the boat parade sail-by," Linda responded, voice tart. "Keeping this community connected is part of the democratic process. That matters, more than any self-indulgent event at the yacht club. I shouldn't have to explain why," she finished, cheeks pink.

Mack sat straight up in his chair, spreading his arms on the table and stretching himself out to full size, once more the hockey enforcer.

"I shouldn't have to remind anyone that the Gasper's Cove boat parade is a major tourist attraction. People like to have a good time, socialize, have a few laughs, and, yes, have a few drinks. Nothing wrong with it. Little more exciting than reading books all summer." He chuckled, pleased with his own humor. "Watch yourself, Linda. Too many computers in the library, and you'll do yourself out of a job. Get Googled into oblivion."

"Googled—good one, Mack," Harry said, surveying the room for appreciation.

Darlene said something unladylike under her breath. Stuart stirred uncomfortably in his seat in front of me and looked out the window. Linda stared ahead, face stiff enough to crack, silent.

"One more item, Mack, then we are done," Maureen said, deliberately oblivious to the tension in the room.

"Right. Heritage?" The warden was ready to move on.

I noticed both Brent and Harry turn toward me, alert. I heard Kenny's metal measuring tape snap. Stuart smiled at me in encouragement.

"Okay. You all know Rankin's, the oldest building in Gasper's Cove." The heads around the table nodded. "Now there's a rumor about a building next to us, but I'm not here to talk about that." Whoever makes the rules wins, I remembered. We'd keep this to what I wanted to talk about—make it pro–protected properties, not antidevelopment. I turned to look at Darlene for support. She avoided my eyes. I continued.

"I am asking the council to look at our building and think about the future." I stopped and handed around the applications the province needed. "I would like you to read these documents, consider them, and then sign them." Frank beamed at me and nudged Linda.

"Once our old buildings, our history, our sense of who we are, is gone"—I couldn't resist looking at Brent—"we'll never get it back."

I sat back down, exhausted. How did politicians do it all day?

The room was quiet. "This is all certainly worth considering," said Mack slowly. "We'll get back to you on this. Now, if that's all? Meeting adjourned."

The warden rose and, almost immediately, chairs scraped as they were pushed away from the table. Moving among his fellow council members, Mack came up to me. He looked behind his shoulder and pulled me aside into a corner of the room.

"Listen. This proposal of yours. I'll talk to the council, but if there is a tie, my vote as warden will carry it. But I have a request. I hear you do a little sewing," he said with a chuckle. "I didn't think people had time for that anymore. Good for you." Mack smiled, clearly assuming he was charming me. "It's about the boat parade. I'm leading the sail. I was thinking of a banner to hang over the side of my boat. Think you could make one for me?"

I could think of nothing I was less interested in doing. A banner. A big, awkward project. What were the dimensions? I'd probably have to appliqué letters on nylon, which could get tricky. How many letters? Could I use pins? Would I have to use grommets?

Mack waited, knowing this was the last thing I wanted to do, but also knowing I'd give in and do it.

"Happy to," I said, putting out my hand and looking the warden right in his bloodshot eyes, aware I was making a gentleman's agreement with a man who was no gentleman at all. "We have a deal."

"Great," Mack said, pleased. "And about this thing of yours with the store. Don't give it another thought, Val. I'll take care of everything. I know exactly what to do."

CHAPTER TEN

I was getting into my car after the meeting when Noah approached me.

"Do you have a minute? I'd like to talk—something about Gerry."

He had my full attention.

"Of course. Do you have a ride? Can I drive you home?" The parking lot was nearly empty.

"That would be good."

"Okay, get in, and we can talk while I drive."

It turned out Noah lived close to me, in a basement apartment he rented from the Smiths—of the Mrs. Smith of the few permed hairs fame. Since their house wasn't far from where we were, Noah and I agreed to drive out along Shore Road for a bit so we could talk. I was reminded suddenly of how I used to do this with the boys when they were teenagers, trapping them in the car with me so I could get them to talk, in a way we often couldn't at home. The scenario was reassuringly familiar.

"What's this about?" I asked, once we were clear of houses and it was just the two of us, the cliffs, the ocean, and the seagulls surfing the air currents.

"You know I went and saw the police, don't you?" he asked.

"I didn't, but that doesn't surprise me. What did they say?"

"I tried to tell them I thought Gerry was onto a story that might have gotten him killed, but that Officer Corkum laughed. He said he knew Gerry, and that Gerry wasn't onto anything more serious than the weather." Looking over, I could see the humiliation in Noah's face; it still hurt. "That guy won't listen to me until I have something solid," he said, staring out of the window at the choppy water.

"Isn't that going to be hard to do?" I asked. "How will you find out something the police can't? The RCMP is working on it."

Noah turned around and looked at me. "You don't understand. I have some notes and some papers. Gerry had this secret hiding place, under the sound tiles."

I remembered the foam egg cartons on the newsroom ceiling. "What did you find?" I asked. We'd driven awhile; I turned around in the look-off parking space.

"Some of it's his own notes, typical Gerry stuff. But the rest are records and credit card receipts. No idea where he got this stuff, but he was hiding it for a reason, so it must be important. The thing is, I don't know what it all means."

"Records and receipts? Maybe expenses?" I suggested. "I had a job once where we had to submit expenses."

"You did?" Noah seemed encouraged. "Could you look at what I found and tell me if there is anything in it I can take to the police?"

I hesitated. What did I know? I wasn't sure if I would be any help, but I didn't have the heart to say no, not to someone so young and so serious.

"Sure. Give me what you have. I'll go over it, but no promises."

"That would be great," Noah said, swallowing. "I have to follow this through, as a journalist."

"I understand," I said, and suddenly missed my own boys—other young men trying to become who they were—so much.

Back in town, Noah ran into the Smith house and returned with two large brown envelopes, not unlike the one Stuart had given me, but these with the town seal on them. I took them and said that if I saw anything suspicious in them, I'd let him know.

After I dropped Noah off, I went and picked up Toby at the store. At the end of a long day, we were both hungry, so as soon as we were home I filled Toby's bowl and opened the fridge to look for leftovers for myself. Somehow, I had to adjust to cooking for one instead of for four. Every time I cooked, it lasted for days. Another skill I had to learn; add it to the list.

Tonight's reheat would be spaghetti. Pasta was my Prozac, and after all that had happened in the last few days, I needed noodles. I microwaved a plate, carried it into the dining room, and dumped the contents of one of Noah's two envelopes onto the table. I could sort through these papers while I ate, and once those were organized, tackle the second envelope while I had my tea.

I made four piles.

The first was for scraps of paper with Gerry's notes, mainly single words followed by question marks.

The second pile was for credit card transactions, the old carbon-copy kind, dating back quite a few years. I wondered how Gerry had gotten these, legally.

Next, I gathered up a stack of standard expense reports, with columns for mileage claims—I recognized those from my brief stint as a courier—and made the third pile. These reports all had the town's logo on them, a lobster and herring intertwined like a crest. I'd have a closer look at those later.

Finally, I made a fourth stack for miscellaneous documents—minutes, agendas, certificates, and a few photocopies of old newspaper articles. Whatever story Gerry had been working on, he was deep into his research when he died.

I decided I would start with the receipts and expense reports. These would involve numbers and would be boring. I'd save Gerry's handwritten notes with the intriguing question marks for later, like dessert.

The expense reports had been submitted by most of the councilors at least five to seven years earlier. I arranged them by person and by date. Of the original councilors, only Harry, Mack, and Frank were still in office. Brent and Linda had joined the council just after the last election, long after these reports had been filed. The largest expenses in front of me were for mileage on "council business" and "UNSM meetings," whatever those were. Next, I went through the credit card receipts. Some of them were for office-type supplies—printer ink and envelopes—but many appeared to be for gas purchases. Because this last group had some correlation with the mileages, I arranged these by date too. Pleased with my uncharacteristic efficiency, I took a break and made tea. Next to the kettle on the counter, I noticed my stack of books from the library. I reached for my phone and dialed.

Catherine picked up. "Hello. Gasper's Cove Public Library."

"Hi. This is Valerie Rankin. Is Linda around?"

"No, I'm the only one who works evenings." Catherine didn't seem too happy with this arrangement. "Is there something I can help you with?"

"I hope so. Linda mentioned Gerry had ordered in some microfiche before he died. She was going to find out what it was. Did she leave anything for me?"

"Let me check. She usually does the interlibrary loans." *Linda did all the interesting jobs,* she implied, *while I, Catherine, work the late shift.*

I waited on the line.

"There are no notes for you, but I can tell you what was on the fiche myself, from looking at the original request. It appears to be for survey maps for the area along the water going up to the fish plant. Make any sense?"

It was time to look at the second, unopened envelope. Once I made sense of the piles already on the table I'd open that one. "Thanks, Catherine. You're a real help, but I have one other question. UNSM? Do those letters mean anything to you? Nova Scotia, but what's the rest of it?"

"Easy," Catherine responded, pleased with herself. "The Union of Nova Scotia Municipalities. They're supposed to keep track of what all the little municipalities and towns are up to. Good luck with that. They have monthly meetings in

Halifax. I know because I have to cover the desk when it's Linda's turn to go."

"Interesting. I won't keep you. Thanks for your help."

"It's what I'm here for." Catherine sighed with resignation and hung up.

Puzzled, I walked over to the fridge and took out milk for my tea. On impulse, I reached for my phone again and tapped in "Union of Nova Scotia Municipalities news."

I was surprised at how many results came up. The UNSM had been around for a long time and had produced a lot of press releases on a variety of topics that didn't interest me. Except one, dated two months ago:

> Starting with the first quarter of the new fiscal year, the UNSM will conduct a rotating audit of municipal administrative costs, following reports of fiscal irregularities incidentally discovered in random audits conducted last year.
>
> "We want to assure the ratepayers of Nova Scotia that we are confident most municipalities have conducted their affairs with the greatest of fiscal responsibility," said Charlie Parker, president of the UNSM. "However, there may be isolated instances where this has not been the case, whether by inaccurate reporting or, in rare circumstances, by intent. This new audit regimen will eliminate any doubt that when municipalities collect taxes, they will then manage them responsibly."

Bingo! We have a winner. *Gerry, you old dog,* I thought, *you were onto something.* I returned to the mass of paper on my dining room table with renewed enthusiasm. Numbers may be boring, but not when they tell a story of human drama.

I reached for the expense reports, the mileage claims in particular, and then the gas receipts. Of the expenses the councilors had submitted, all but Frank had claimed mileage. I wondered why, so I turned my attention to the gas receipts to see if his name was there. It wasn't. I didn't see any name on the receipts. The imprint on all of them was the same, the Town of Gasper's Cove. A corporate credit card. All the councilors must have one. But I had no way of knowing which of the councilors had used the town's card to buy gas.

Frustrated, I next turned to the expenses to see if I could find a pattern.

It didn't take long.

On some reports, those submitted by Harry, the dates on which he'd claimed gas mileage matched the dates on many of the gas receipts. I sat back; this made no sense. Were those his receipts or not? Or were they from another councilor who had traveled the same day? My head ached, and I tried to remember the forms I had filled out as a courier. Had I submitted both mileage and gas receipts? I didn't think so. Then I remembered why. When receipts were handed in, the amounts were simply reimbursed. Mileage reports were different. Those were paid at a set rate. What was it years ago, 56 cents a mile? I remembered this extra was added to paychecks at the end of the month, and it always felt like a bonus.

I got up and walked around the house. Aunt Dot's salt and pepper shakers needed a dust. She'd have a fit if she saw them now. I was slipping—too much on my mind for good housekeeping. The home was a time warp, with avocado-green appliances in the kitchen, a pink tub and toilet in the bathroom, and a chenille spread on the bed. I was glad my aunt had left everything the way it was when she moved down south. I was snug and secure in this little bungalow— exactly as I remembered from my childhood. Its consistency gave me breathing room in which to figure out how to lead a life on my own again, now that my children didn't need me the same way anymore. An uneasy thought passed through my mind. What if the innocent town I'd left and tried to return to wasn't the same anymore? Was this what the papers on the dining room table were trying to say?

No, there had to be an obvious answer to Gerry's puzzles, maybe not obvious to me. I went over to the big, comfortable chair in the living room and moved Toby over so I could fit in next to him. Tight up against the big dog I picked up some knitting. I had a raglan summer sweater to get done before the season arrived. I knit and thought, knit and thought, moving my mind back and forth between my stitches and the numbers and dates on Gerry's papers, slowing down only for the CDD.

I stopped and stared at my needles. CDD, center double decrease. Double cross, double dipping. I got up and went back to the dining room.

This was what Gerry had seen.

Since the dates on Harry's mileage claims and the dates on the gas receipts matched, it looked like the councilor could have used a credit card to buy gas, and then claimed mileage too, as an expense. There were a lot of miles listed, back and forth, to those UNSM meetings in Halifax, and it looked like Harry had been paid for them twice. As a scheme, it was unethical but both simple and complicated, likely to be discovered only by an alert supervisor, a provincial audit, or a wily old radio guy.

What next?

I could go to the RCMP with this, but then Wade and Nolan would want to know where I got the information. If I told them it had come from Noah, would he get into trouble for withholding documents from the police? That would not be, I suspected, a good start to a journalistic career.

Plus, what I had in front of me on my dining room table was more theory than evidence. Numbers had never been my best thing, but then again, being paid had always mattered to me and I had always been precise about cash. There might be another reasonable explanation, but something told me there wasn't. If I was right about Harry's own CDD, I needed to know how double dipper Harry, if that's what he was, had gotten away with it. Who should have caught it? Who'd signed off on the expenses? Someone always did, I remembered. I pulled the papers closer and searched for the inevitable "Approved by."

There it was, a scrawled "MM."

Mack McRae.

If Harry had been scamming the council, he hadn't done it alone; he'd had help. Gerry knew it, I knew it, and so did whoever had passed this information on to a reporter.

Gerry, it seemed, wasn't the only one with enemies.

CHAPTER ELEVEN

The next evening, I was back at the store to get ready for my "Tailoring for the Timid" class. We were behind schedule, due to some interfacing distraction (most of it had been fused upside down onto the iron), but we were plowing ahead, with a plan that evening to do a frontal attack on welt pockets and hope for the best. If we didn't get moving, those jackets would leave at the end of the session without linings. It was a lot of pressure.

Once in the classroom, I pulled out my samples and sat at the machine. Like many women, my students worked from the instructions, my suggestions, and what their hands told them. I knew that the more samples, in different stages, I prepared, the faster they'd figure out the pockets. But as soon as I lifted the presser foot, I could see the machine wasn't how I'd left it. Someone had loosened the tension, and worse, there was now black thread in the bobbin. Every good sewing teacher knows it's hard to see stitches in black; I always used turquoise for my samples. I wondered what had happened, particularly because we locked the classroom between classes, and had ever since two small boys almost pulled the water tank for the iron down from the ceiling and onto their giggling little bodies.

I poked my head out of the classroom door. Duck was near the cash register.

"Hey, Duck, has anyone been in the classroom lately?" I called out. Quiet, and as soft on his feet as Shadow the cat, Duck didn't miss much. If anyone had been in the room, he'd know.

He hesitated and looked at a space over my head. "Nope, only me to sweep. Like I'm supposed to."

"Okay, it's something with the machine. Losing my mind, I guess." I could see some of my early students were arriving. It was time to get to work. "Talk to you later."

Stepping back into the classroom, I got busy helping the women set up, finding plugs for the machines, and making sure everyone had enough room to lay out projects. When I got to her table, Sarah Chisholm pulled me aside.

Looking around to make sure no one was listening, she whispered, "Guess they're treating Gerry's death as suspicious. Medical evidence." Sarah worked at the hospital, something to do with making artificial limbs. She prided herself on inside knowledge and enjoyed sharing it.

"Really?" I said. Maybe Noah was right. "I thought it was a fall."

"No. I have a friend who works in the basement." My confusion showed on my face. "You know, the morgue?"

"Right. So how do they know it wasn't an accident?"

"He had a bruise on his hip and smaller ones along one side. The police went back to the scene and took measurements of the door. They figure someone slammed it on him, and the knob caught him on the hip, and the door hit him on the side." Sarah gave me a knowing look. "The measurements match. They think it stunned him, he went forward, and maybe was even pushed. By the time he hit the bottom, his neck was broken." Sarah seemed satisfied with this scenario.

"So, it was murder?"

"That's what a suspicious death usually means," Sarah said with authority. "Of course, this is confidential, and you didn't hear it from me. My friend could get in trouble."

"Won't breathe a word," I said, wondering how many people Sarah had already told. The papers littering my table at home suddenly seemed more important.

"I heard you on the radio with him, so thought you should know," Sarah said. "Guess you want to get the class going but thought you'd be interested."

⌒☌⌒

Sarah's news shocked me. It was hard to pull my mind back to sewing, but I knew my students needed me to facilitate an interesting night out as much as they needed my teaching. The drama of family life, immediate and extended, was as central to my curriculum as collars, facings, and buttonholes. As I went from table to table, helping students, I listened to the conversation while my hands worked with pins and fabric.

"Shame about Gerry."

"I can't believe I've put the same sleeve in twice, in the wrong armhole."

"I do that all the time. They say he was dead before he went down the stairs."

"Val, do I have to unpick this? If I cry, will you do it for me?"

"If that's Charlie calling about warming the bottle again, I'm not picking up."

"Do you believe there's going to be another election?"

"Walter's retired now. Goes and sits at the table every day at noon, waiting for his lunch."

"Now you're together all the time. Gets hard."

"No kidding. I can't get a thing done."

"Why does the bobbin always run out before the end of the seam?"

"Didn't we just have one?"

"What election? Who votes?"

"My sister-in-law got extensions. It looks better than you'd think."

"Check the bobbin before you start. Wind an extra one."

"Not an accident, for sure. Don't you think, Sarah?"

"Mack's going to run again. Count on it."

"Does anyone have scissors I can borrow?"

"This machine would sew better if I plugged it in, wouldn't it?"

"What about Harry? Council's most money he ever had."

"Good one. My mom wants to know about the co-op, Val. Are you taking jam?"

"Does this look right to you? Mack's still a hotshot in his mind."

"Love your mom's rhubarb jam. Can't buy it—got to make it."

"Who? Are we still talking about Mack or Harry?"

"Is this iron too hot? You mean down the stairs?"

"Exactly."

And so it went for two and a half hours, until we stopped at eight-thirty, with some of the jackets, amazingly, further along than expected. As I packed up, Duck came into the classroom to sweep up the thread and empty the trash cans. As I watched him work, I realized I knew little about the criminal mind. I'd ease into this.

"Can I ask you a question?" I started. "Do you know any of the folks on the town council?"

"Sure." Duck was cautious. "See them in the store, time to time."

"I know this sounds crazy, but did you notice anything about any of them? You know, anything that might make you think they weren't quite on the straight and narrow."

Duck eyed me calmly. "You asking if any of them are crooked, because I'm the guy who's been in jail, and so I would know?"

"I wasn't thinking that at all," I said. He'd seen right through me. "I thought you might have an opinion if they are up to something."

Duck sighed and leaned his broom up against the wall. "So you think there are criminals on the council, and you are wondering who they are." He wasn't asking a question but stating a fact. This was exactly what I wanted to know.

"I don't like to talk about people, but if it stays between you and me ..." He paused. "You and Rollie been decent."

"Anything you can tell me, I'd appreciate. My lips are sealed," I said, making a zipping motion across my mouth. Duck knew something. I wanted to know what.

"All right. Harry. The first guy I'd think of." Duck bent to pick up a bird's nest of thread from the floor. "One time, I saw him peeling off a price tag from a cheap snow shovel and sticking it on the handle of one of the expensive ones. Kids' stuff. Who didn't do that in high school?"

Me. I didn't do it. I was sure Darlene hadn't either.

"I know he lives with his mother, but he could still be short of money. A guy like that probably would be."

"What do you mean?"

"He's got the face. Maybe behind in his support payments, VLTs—just saying."

I did a quick translation in my head. VLTs, those video lottery machines in corner stores and the casino.

"Anyone else?" I was enjoying this. Duck was a great guy to talk to about sneaky stuff.

"That car guy, Brent. Wouldn't trust him as far as I could throw him. But he's got his dad's money behind him. They all do, not that it'd mean anything. The old man's tougher than he is. Might cut him off." Duck stopped. "This is about money, am I right? Trouble usually is."

I couldn't share the information I had at home in my dining room, so I nodded.

"What about the warden, or Linda from the library, or Frank?" I might as well try to get as much out of Duck as I could.

"I wouldn't want to say anything about the minister; you'd have to ask someone else about him. All I can tell you is he was in one time looking for those bike clips things for pant legs. Said he doesn't drive. Everybody drives." Duck thought it over. "Do you think it could be one of those religious things?"

"I doubt it. Last time I checked, the United Church had nothing against driving. That's the Old Order Mennonites."

"Yeah, right." Duck waited for another question. I wondered how long it had been since anyone had asked his opinion on anything.

"So Linda and the warden?" I coaxed. "Anything strike you there?" This was getting interesting.

"That lady from the library is nice, in a library kind of way. Don't read much. There's one thing ..." He moved closer to me. "Figure there's history there. She can't stand Mack and takes off down a different aisle if she sees him. It's not like it's about something new. Kind of mad you get about something that happened a long time ago, and still getting to you. You know?"

I met his eyes. We both knew the feeling.

"What does the warden think about her?"

"No clue. He seems happy. His wife's Brent's sister. Pretty sure big brother helps them out. Mack runs a tab here, stuff for the boat. Cruises in, loads up the car, the wife comes in end of the month and settles up. Good deal for Mack. But that's all there is."

The bell on the store's front door rang, and a late customer came into the store. Duck and I moved apart. He returned to pushing his wide broom across the floor; I retreated to my sewing classroom.

Duck had gone up in my estimation. For someone who didn't like to gossip, he was good at it.

No one knows what info lurks in the minds of clerks.

This was progress. I had a good idea of what was going on at the council. All I had to do was prove it.

CHAPTER TWELVE

Inspired by my conversation with Duck, I texted Noah. I had an evening reconnaissance mission to go on, and this one needed a partner.

> It's late, but are you up for a short run over to Drummond?

OK why?

> About those papers. Will explain.
> Meet me in front of the store.

I straightened up and locked the classroom, grabbed my purse, and left. Noah was walking down the sidewalk, and I went to meet him. He had on creased jeans and a rumpled shirt, with a messenger bag over his shoulder. No one irons anymore and no one minds.

"Hey, what's up?" he said, curious. Evening calls from middle-aged women weren't a normal part of his routine.

"Hi! Thanks for coming. It's about those expense reports. It looks to me like there's been some messing around with the mileage claims. Plus, someone suggested Harry might be pressed for cash, maybe gambling, VLTs."

Noah pulled his head back with surprise. "Okay, so what do you want me to do? Not sure I follow."

"This is the thing ... The RCMP will want more. I have to check out Harry. We need to find VLTs, so where do we go?"

"I don't know. Not my thing. Check out the casino over in Drummond? That what you're thinking?"

"It is." I hoped this nice kid didn't think I was completely wacko. "It's the last Thursday of the month. Government checks go out." I'd once worked payroll at the Port Authority. "Maybe see if Harry is in there, or find someone to tell us if he goes there a lot."

"I get it. Sort of. But you want me to come with you ... why?"

"Look. We need to case the joint." I couldn't believe I just said that. "It would look weird for someone like me to be alone in a place like that, but a young guy, it would be easier. It will take two of us, anyway. One on the inside, one to see if he goes in and out. You know—watch the entrances."

Noah had a look on his face like he was thinking maybe I watched too much TV. He might be right.

"Why not? It can't hurt, and besides, at least we're doing something. We can go over, and I'll go in. But first I need you to explain exactly what you found in those papers."

"Deal." I was relieved he'd agreed to help, so, on the drive over the causeway, I told him about Harry's gas scheme.

"I get why you want to know more about Harry. I do. But there're a couple of things I don't get."

In the passenger seat beside me, my partner's face was serious.

"Like what?"

"For a start, why would the warden be enabling Harry's scam?"

"I don't know. Maybe he was getting a cut? He owed him something? It would be good to find that out, but we have to start somewhere."

Noah sighed. "Agreed, but the big question is ... is this why Gerry was killed? Over some shady gas receipts? I mean, really? Hardly worth it."

"I know what you're saying," I agreed. "But here's my logic. Gerry knew something big enough to get killed over. You're right—probably something bigger than this. We don't know what. But this expense part looks crooked. To me, it's a crack in the door, a way into learning more, finding out what else was going on." I thought about Duck's story about the price tags; details could always mean something bigger. "We need to start with Harry because he's the weakest link. If we can get a solid sense of what's going on, we can turn it over to the RCMP. They can take it from there."

Noah looked at me speculatively. "Are you sure you're not a reporter?"

I laughed. "Nope, that's about the only job I've never done. Just born nosy."

The Drummond Casino was a black-walled brick building on the edge of town. It had been set up as a provincial/municipal project years ago, ostensibly to increase tourism but really as just another attempt to bring in tax dollars.

Since then, the casino had been a source of the occasional how-I-lost-my-house kind of news story, and so now it tried to keep a low profile. There was a small neon sign out front, posters on responsible gaming and "don't drink and drive" on either side of the revolving doors, and two ATMs inside the front entrance.

Once we arrived, I doubted my plan. It was likely this was the misdirected mission of a sewing teacher trying to be a detective. Still, I had brought Noah this far. We might as well follow through.

I pulled up near the back of the building, out of sight of the entrance, to brief my accomplice.

"This shouldn't take long. Have a walk around; see if Harry's in there, or ask about him. If it turns out he's a gambler, we may be onto something."

Noah got out of the car, then paused, his hand on the handle of the door. "Got it, chief; will report back."

While I waited, I pulled out my phone and checked my messages. More offers of handicrafts for the co-op. Someone named Skylar had socks with hand-painted yarn—this intrigued me—and someone named Dolores had kitchen towels with crocheted tops that could be buttoned up and hung on the oven door and, she said, looked real nice.

I slumped in my seat, overwhelmed. Inventory would not be my problem. All I needed now was a rent-free space on a floor that wouldn't collapse, in a building that wouldn't fall down. Completely possible if I could get a group of councilors who were all probably crooks to declare our store a heritage site. In my spare time, I had to sew a boat banner and figure out why a radio guy who knew about my scheme had been murdered the day he met me.

I put my head down on the steering wheel. I wasn't making sense, even to myself.

Across the street, a door opened, letting out light, music, and customers. I lifted my head and looked over. I saw three people I knew. One was Brent Cameron, laughing and slapping the back of an hilarious Lars Nyberg. A few paces behind them was Stuart Campbell, walking with a thin blonde about my age, in high wobbly sandals and a purple polyester print dress. His wife?

Brent and Lars turned and crossed the street toward me. I scrunched down into my seat, but not before Brent made eye contact. Why had I parked under the streetlight? I was such an amateur. Passing by my car, he rapped lightly on my rear fender. He knew I was up to no good.

Letting out a sigh at my detective ineptitude, I snuck a look back over at Stuart and the woman. They seemed to be saying goodbye. I was no expert in body language, but it looked awkward. The woman reached out several times to touch Stuart playfully on the arm, and he stood stiffly, his hands in his pockets. Finally, after a few minutes in which they both stood in silence, they turned and walked away in different directions. Not a wife. Had I just observed our engineer on an unsuccessful date? This was interesting, very interesting.

Still processing the encounter, and asking myself why I was so interested in Stuart's private life, I didn't hear the handle on the passenger side of the door click. Startled, I realized Noah had returned from his mission. He slid into the seat beside me, a look of both triumph and concern on his face.

"Drive, drive, drive," he said. "I don't want them to see us. You were right." He looked over at me with amazement. "Mr. Harry, the councilor, got thrown out of the casino. They cut him off. Had to call someone to get picked up. And guess who showed up?"

"Tell me, tell me!" This was all coming together, making sense.

"I hate to say it, but it was your cousin Darlene."

CHAPTER THIRTEEN

Once we were back in Gasper's Cove, I dropped Noah off and went home. We'd been quiet after we'd left the casino. Clearly, my surveillance partner was as encouraged by our evening out as I was discouraged.

Darlene wasn't his cousin.

I hadn't said much to him about her; I didn't know what to think myself. What had she gotten herself into? One thing was certain. I wouldn't be turning over any of Gerry's documents to the police, or sharing my suspicions about Harry, until I talked to her first.

What an evening.

I was tired, so once home, rather than taking Toby out for a late-night walk, I let him loose in the backyard, with apologies. Watching him through the window over the sink, I filled the kettle and then went into the dining room to revisit Gerry's papers. The expense reports had told their story. I turned to the handwritten notes. Maybe I would find some answers there.

Gerry's papers were a mess. His handwriting was worse than mine. He had scrawled on cocktail napkins, on the back of fast-food receipts, on lined pages torn from notebooks, and even on a piece of cardboard that appeared to be torn from a cereal box—Cap'n Crunch. *Poor Gerry*, I thought, while I tried to sift this paper rubble into some kind of order. *What a life you lived.*

Fortunately, as disordered as his documentation had been, Gerry had been a skilled user of punctuation. So rather than by date, I sorted his notes into groups by question mark, by star, and by exclamation mark. From these, I pushed aside "buy new socks (!)," "change oil in the car (?)," and "return empties (★)." But what was he looking for with "Survey (★!)"? And why was there a question mark after Linda's name and "dirt (!!?)"? Dirt on who? The only useful information, and undoubtedly done during breakfast or late at night, was a sort of diagram, drawn on the inside of the piece of cardboard. It looked like the solar system: one big circle in the middle, with a dollar sign in it, and a series of little circles, with the names of the councilors, plus some of the town employees, like Kenny, rotating around it. A few of the names—Harry, Frank, and Mack—had arrows connecting their planets to the dollar-sign sun. What did all this mean? I wished I could talk to Gerry and make sense of it.

Frustrated, I got up, let Toby in, and made a second cup of tea. My phone dinged. A message from Duck.

Boss accident. At ER.

What? What happened?

I waited. No answer. I waited. After ten more minutes of silence, the sick feeling in my stomach was more than I could stand, and so for the second time that night, I drove across the causeway.

I made it to the Drummond Consolidated Regional Hospital in record time, pulled through the U-shaped driveway sheltered by the Emergency overhang, parked in the closest visitor's spot, and hurried to the entrance. I was through the automatic doors almost before they had time to open.

I ran up to the triage nurse at the front desk.

"I'm here for Rollie. Where is he? What happened? Is he okay?"

The nurse paused, the skin tightening around her mouth as if she were thinking of the right thing to say. "Honestly, I think this is something you should see for yourself."

That did not sound good.

"Rollie and Duck are in exam room B waiting for the doctor with the machine." She stifled a giggle. "I'll buzz you through."

Machine? What was she talking about?

"Okay, thanks. See you later," I called out as I turned away from her. The second set of sliding doors opened.

I found room B and knocked. There was no answer. Tentatively, I pushed against the heavy door.

The nurse was right. What was in the tiny room was something no one could describe. High on the narrow table, his usually florid face the same color as the off-white hospital walls, Rollie sat, cradling my classroom sewing machine in his lap. Looking closer, I was shocked to see my cousin wasn't simply holding the machine; it was attached to him—the thumb of his right hand firmly impaled by the machine's sharp needle, a #14 jeans, sharp. It hurt me just to look at it.

I wasn't the only one who felt queasy. Off in the corner of the room, Duck was perched on a small plastic chair, his head between his knees. He was doing the kind of deep breathing they say will keep you from throwing up but almost never does.

"What happened?" An obvious question. I waited for the answer. That was my good machine.

"We were trying things out," Rollie said between clenched teeth. "Obviously, we didn't know what we were doing."

Duck shook his head in the corner. "Sorry, boss. So sorry." It looked like he had sewn right through Rollie's thumb. Quite the team.

The door behind me clicked, and a young doctor walked into the room, nodded to me, noted Duck in the corner, and turned to Rollie. "What have we here?"

"Stitched through my hand," Rollie said, wincing, trying hard to be polite despite his pain.

The doctor paused, absorbed the situation, and then reached over and loosened the screw on the needle bar, freeing Rollie's hand from the machine.

"My mother sewed. You know you didn't need to drive over with the whole machine. That must have been tough over some of those potholes. We'll pull that needle out and get it all cleaned up. Have you had your tetanus shot?"

"No idea," Rollie said, as the doctor carefully and gently moved the injured thumb out from under the presser foot and set the heavy machine down onto the floor. Duck looked over and groaned.

This was enough for me. I had no desire to see the needle being removed or to watch Rollie get his shot.

"Listen. I'll take the machine out, put it in the car," I said, waving Duck aside as he made a weak attempt to stand and help me. Lifting the machine into my arms, I marched out through the waiting room and nearly bumped into Sarah Chisholm from my class.

"Here—let me help you. Looks heavy," Sarah said, taking the foot control from my hand and following me out into the parking lot. "I had to do a presentation to the hospital board tonight—you know, more funding. All the town busybodies. What a tough crowd. Just wait till they need a prosthesis." She looked sideways at me, assessing my mood. "I'm just sorry I didn't see the guys when they came in. It's all around the hospital." She tried to suppress a giggle and failed.

"I can only imagine," I said as we arrived at my car. "What a couple of knuckleheads. I don't know what they were thinking."

"No kidding." Sarah handed me the foot control. "Maybe you should sign them up for classes."

She was still laughing as she left me to go across the lot to her car, talking on her phone as she walked, no doubt making sure all of Gasper's Cove knew about Rollie's accident.

What could I do? I popped the trunk, hoisted the machine into it, and slammed it shut. If Duck and Rollie wanted to sew, why didn't they ask me for help first?

When I returned to the ER, Rollie's thumb was wrapped in gauze, and he was receiving his discharge instructions. "Try to keep it dry for a day or two, but I think you're out of the woods now. Next time, take out the needle before you get in the car," the doctor said, working hard to keep his mouth in a straight line as he walked away to attend to real emergencies.

Duck stared at the blank hospital wall. He'd let the boss down. I should have felt sorry for the pair of them but didn't.

"Mending," Rollie started. "We were mending."

"Mending? I don't know what to say." For once in my life this was true. "We can talk about the consequences of sewing, on my good machine, without supervision later. I'm done. I'm going home to be with Toby. Right now, he's the only one in this entire community who has any common sense, and that's not a lot."

With that, I left them—my cousin, bandaged and contrite, and his accomplice—at the door of the hospital. I got in my car and drove off, a bloodied sewing machine in my trunk, and nothing but unanswered questions in my head.

CHAPTER FOURTEEN

The next morning, Toby and I took our time at home. I dusted the Royal Doulton figurines on the mantel, watered the African violets, and repositioned the ashtrays no one had used in 40 years to their spots on the end tables. Toby followed me around the L-shaped living room, fascinated by the novelty of watching me clean and attentive to my muttering. I was in no hurry to see Rollie or Duck but felt a growing urgency to track down Darlene. She had some explaining to do. However, all my calls went straight to voicemail, on both her cell and her work phones. I left messages.

It seemed the entire world had put me on hold. I had no idea if the council was signing off on the heritage request. There was no response from Julie about Lars Nyberg, and now even Darlene was avoiding me.

Discouraged and feeling hard done by, I picked up my duster and attacked the salt and pepper shakers next, but even the kissing Dutch boy and girl and pairs of poodles and flamingos couldn't cheer me up.

Eventually, I gave up trying to distract myself and I went back to the dining room table. I picked up the second of Gerry's envelopes. Reaching inside, I pulled out four sheets. Each was labeled "Topographical survey," followed by lot numbers and coordinates, all of which, apart from the big "N," which I assumed meant north, were completely meaningless to me. Still, there was something vaguely familiar about them. I had seen this recently. But where? Of course. The survey maps on the walls of Stuart's office. I bet he could interpret these for me.

How could I ask him? I'd only seen him three times, once at an awkward and discouraging meeting about the store, once at the back of the room at the council meeting, and once at a distance with some woman on the street. Hardly the basis for a working relationship. How weird would it be if I called him out of nowhere and asked for a favor? And even if he agreed to look at the surveys, would he charge me for his time? I couldn't afford that. Plus, if he asked me where I got these papers, what would I say? That they had been found behind some foam egg cartons in the ceiling of a radio station where a newsman had been murdered?

More to the point, what would I say if he asked, as I was sure he would, why I was talking to him instead of the police?

I didn't have good answers to any of these questions.

It was settled. I'd depend on my charm. I found my purse, dug out Stuart's card, and dialed.

"Campbell," he said, answering on the first ring. Must be a slow day in the office.

"Stuart, glad to catch you." People liked you to think they were busy even when they weren't; I learned that in the service industry. "Valerie Rankin here. Listen—I owe you one." Of course, I had no idea what for, but I also knew from hospitality that most people usually felt underappreciated. "I'd like to take you out for coffee. Soon."

Stuart sounded suspicious. "Is this a social call, or is it about my report? I talked to Rollie. He knows you can't do anything upstairs."

"It's under control. Rollie's been caught up in things." That was one way of putting it.

"Great. Anything back from the council on the historic building angle?"

"No, not yet. Thought I'd check with them at the end of the week. Mack thinks it will be okay."

"Good. Getting the property protected would solve a lot of problems for you." There was silence on the other end of the phone. "Now, what do you really want?"

Rats. So much for charm. Neither of us had any, apparently.

"I have papers, survey-type papers, and I want to know what they mean. They may be important," I finished lamely.

Stuart laughed. "And you want my professional opinion, but you only want to pay for a coffee to get it?"

"Pretty much." The blonde the other night was smart to walk away, I thought.

"Okay, let's say four p.m. at the place downstairs. Get me a large double-double."

Two creams, two sugars? A man after my own heart.

"You got it."

I had a date.

Stuart was on time for our meeting; I'd just ordered coffee when he arrived. I'd taken a booth at the back, near the door to the kitchen, away from the window.

It took him a minute to see me, and when he did, he nodded and glanced at his watch and sat down.

"This won't take long. I appreciate it," I said.

"No, not at all. Just making sure I have time to pick up my daughter. You have kids?"

"Grown and flown. All away. One son working in New York, one is in Toronto, and a daughter is in school in Scotland. They'll probably never move back to Nova Scotia. But they love Gasper's. We used to come down in the summers when they were kids. I'll see more of them here than if I stayed in the city, I know that. They're coming home for a visit this summer. I want to show them their mother is doing something interesting."

I stopped, shocked. I'd said something to this man I hadn't articulated even to myself.

"The crafters' co-op?" he asked.

"Yes, the co-op. It was all I could think of." I felt like a fool.

Stuart looked at me quietly. "You must have had your kids very young. Never would have guessed," he said. "I was close to 40, so here I am with an almost teenager and trying to keep up." He shook his head. "It's more complicated than it used to be."

"So true. No internet before."

"She and I manage. She's a good kid," he said. The topic was over. "Now, what's this about?"

I pulled the papers from my purse and spread them out on the table between us.

Stuart picked them up and noted the name of the surveyor at the bottom. "Handley. He retired quite a while ago. Where did you get these?" He took out some wire-framed glasses and put them on.

"Oh, around the house. Wanted to know if they were important or if I should throw them out."

Stuart raised his eyebrows and wiggled them. The message was clear—he wasn't buying it. Even so, he couldn't resist the excitement of a survey drawing.

"Interesting."

"What is it?"

Stuart reached over and unwrapped a cutlery bundle from the edge of the table. Using a knife, he pointed to rows of lines that waved across the paper.

"This is a topographical survey of the area between the fish plant and the road on your side of the water." He laid the sheets together so I could see they were segments of a larger piece of land. "It shows the relative areas of elevation." He looked over at me. "You know, where the ground is flat and where it isn't? These surveys are done before construction. Standard practice."

Seemed dull to me. "But you said it was interesting. What did you mean?"

Stuart examined the drawings. "This looks to me like the survey they would have done before the new road went in. What's interesting is, based on what I see here, they ended up putting the road closer to the water than I would have recommended."

I was losing the train of the conversation, I just wanted to know what the surveys meant. Getting something out of this guy wasn't easy.

"Why?"

"Looking at this, putting in the road was a lot more work and expense than it had to be. They should have gone straight in here." He traced a route with the knife. "Pretty simple. But this," he said, pointing at the edge of the middle paper, "tells me that where they ended up building required a heck of a lot of fill and a lot more money. It doesn't make sense."

Now, even I was interested. I remembered Harry had been involved at the fish plant. Maybe this was important; I needed to know more, but I had to go at this sideways— work around this guy's logical mind.

"Let's forget the topography for a moment. The what, and the why." I was hoping Stuart would get to what I needed to know. "I'm interested in the who."

Stuart leaned back in the booth and studied me over the top of his glasses. He wasn't following me at all.

"Who would have decided where the road would be built?" I asked, nursing him along.

"Council, I guess. They'd have to approve funds," Stuart said, appraising me. "Vote for it."

"Say the council went for this. Would they understand they authorized something more expensive?"

"Not necessarily. It depends on how it was presented to them. I mean, I had to explain it to you."

I let that pass. I had an idea forming in the back of my mind. Gerry must have seen this, too.

"So, this didn't benefit the taxpayer. Who would have gained something from the road being built where it was?"

Stuart shrugged. "Any number of people would be my guess. Someone who wanted a new road near the water,

I suppose. Someone with a lot of fill to get rid of. The land belonged to the plant, but not sure why they'd care where the road was. They wouldn't have paid for it." He paused. "What's really going on here? You're asking a lot of questions."

"I'm trying to put something together, help a friend."

A phone buzzed in Stuart's pocket. I watched his face as he read a text.

He sighed. "Do you know where I can get embroidery floss? My daughter is mixed up in some nutty money-making project. I guess it's harmless, but we've got stuff all over the house. It's driving me crazy."

"I have tons of floss at home. I'll never use it all. I'm more into garment sewing and knitting myself. I can drop a bag off if you like." I knew what it was like to be caught up in a project and run out of materials. There was nothing worse.

That smile again. "Would you do that? I'd appreciate it. Thanks for the coffee." The smile faded, and Stuart put his phone back into his pocket and stood. "Whatever you're into, good luck. And maybe"—he hesitated—"watch your-self. Road construction can be a dirty business. In more ways than one."

CHAPTER FIFTEEN

After my coffee with Stuart, I went back to the store and looked for Rollie. I found him at the counter sorting mail, hindered slightly by his bandaged thumb and by Shadow, who walked delicately across the bills with her small, perfect feet, making the point once again that nothing should go on if it didn't include cats. Given the way he was the last time I saw him, I was surprised to see Rollie cheerful.

"I talked to the bank. Stuart was right; your plan might work. If we can get the province involved, the bank will lend us enough for the renovations. Why didn't we think about becoming a historical property sooner? How did you come up with this?"

"Creative thinking motivated by lack of resources. The story of my life. Besides, a building whispered to me." I knew what I had to say next; it was hanging between us. "Now, about last night."

"Not one of my finer moments," Rollie admitted. "The real injury was to my pride. Duck's still getting over it. It won't happen again."

My cousin was hiding something from me, which was not like him at all, and I could feel it. "This was the first time you've done any mending," I said, hoping to draw him out. Rollie picked up a stack of work gloves and stared at them, fascinated. I waited, and when he continued to ignore me, I turned away. "In future, if you want to know how to sew, just ask me."

"Will do," Rollie said, eager to change the subject. "One more thing. Can you see Polly before you go? She's been in the office for an hour at the printer. She wants to talk to you."

I stopped at the office on my way out to the car. When I opened the door, Polly was waiting for me, sitting behind Rollie's desk, which, I saw, she'd cleaned.

"Valerie," the twelve-year-old said. "Please come in. I think we should have a meeting."

"Of course. I understand you've been printing. A school project?"

Polly was offended. "No. A business plan. Can I get you water?" She reached forward and handed me a neatly clipped stack of paper. She had a large, loose, adult watch on her slim wrist.

I read.

Polly had prepared a product description for embroidery floss friendship bracelets, a production schedule, a cost analysis, a market research summary (the market for friendship bracelets in Gasper's Cove was far from saturated), and a plan for both social media and conventional marketing.

On the last page of her packet were the pictures of two girls, Polly herself and a second girl who seemed familiar.

She watched my face intently as I read.

"You've done a lot of work here," I said. "I'm impressed." I was, too. It must be hard to be a middle-aged MBA trapped in a preteen body. "So you and your friend," I read, "Erin Campbell, are planning on making friendship bracelets for the co-op. Is that right?"

"We have the expertise; we know the market." Polly leaned forward, and I saw the elastics on the braces on her teeth. "We're thinking of launching locally here, reaching out to tourists during the summer, then moving to wider distribution by no later than the third quarter. Maybe branching out to bookmarks—they're big. It's all on page four of the report. I have a slide deck here," she said, holding up a pink flash drive, "but Rollie's desktop doesn't have PowerPoint, if you can believe that."

I was surprised Rollie's computer even had power, but there was no point in bringing that up now.

"No, it's fine. I get the idea from this report." I held up the sheaf of papers. "I am sure we don't have anyone else making bracelets, so when we get up and running, we'll put some out for sale for sure." I smelled strawberry and noticed a layer of lip gloss on Polly's mouth.

"Excellent," Polly said, unzipping her backpack and extracting a large plastic bag of thin, woven bands. "I have some prototypes. Beta testing." She pushed the bag toward me.

"Thanks," I said, and then, on an impulse, reached forward to shake her hand. "I think we can do business."

Behind the big desk, Polly beamed at me.

After my business meeting, I took Polly's bag of beta bracelets to the classroom, acutely aware my life was running on two tracks. On one hand, I had unleashed the creative hopes of an unexpected number of people, old and young, and on the other, my mind was full of thoughts of roads, expense scams, and murder. What did I think I was doing? What happened to my plan to sit in my aunt's house, walk my dog, and sell crafts? Lost in my thoughts, I walked to the back of the store, heading toward the back exit and my car. While I was here, I should get the machine into the classroom.

I went down the back stairs and walked to the car, turned my key in the lock, and lifted the lid of the trunk. I reached down to lift the heavy machine out.

My trunk was empty. No machine. Not there. Just not there.

My mind knew my eyes were wrong. I had loaded the machine, minus its needle, into the trunk of this car last night in the parking lot of the Drummond Consolidated Regional Hospital.

Was I losing it? Carefully, I lowered the lid of the trunk, took a deep breath, and then lifted it again. The machine still wasn't there. I went to the front of the car and peered in. I saw a bag of interfacing on the back seat, a matted dog brush, and some chocolate almonds spilled on the floor up front. The car was mine.

I tried to think.

Where was my machine? What had happened after I had left the hospital?

I had driven home and gone to bed. The car had spent the night in my driveway, except for the hour it was parked in front of the Peking Duck, while I had coffee with the distracted, attractive, and somewhat informative Stuart Campbell.

Had my car been locked? In Drummond, probably; at home, probably not. In Gasper's Cove, we didn't lock our houses, much less our cars. I doubted if I even knew where the house key my aunt had given me was. Then I remembered the trunk release button to the left of the brake pedal on the floor. Anyone could have walked down the driveway, reached in, and popped the trunk. Someone had been at my house during the night and taken my sewing machine, while Toby and I slept in our bed. The thought made me nauseous.

This was more than I could handle on my own. I dialed the RCMP office. Officer Nolan was out on highway duty. I was put through to Wade.

"Corkum."

"Hi, Wade. It's Valerie. I have some things to report."

"Like what?"

"First, my sewing machine has been stolen."

"Excuse me?"

"Out of the trunk. I put it into the car at the hospital, and now it's not there."

"Oh yeah, last night." I heard Wade snicker in my ear. "I heard your cousin had a little accident. It's all over town."

"Yes, he did. He's fine. But my machine is gone."

"That right? Have you checked everywhere? Maybe left it somewhere because you were, well, upset, over there at the hospital? I understand it was quite a scene." Wade was having fun with this.

"Listen, Wade. This machine is big, heavy, and it's gone. No, I didn't leave it somewhere by mistake and can't remember. I'm trying to report a theft."

"Consider it done." Wade was crisp, remembering he was an officer of the law, not just someone I knew from high school. "I suggest you contact your insurance adjustor. It's probably covered under your household policy."

"Wait—that's not all."

"Don't tell me you lost your scissors too." Wade thought he was hilarious.

"No. But I have some papers that I think are linked to Gerry's death."

"Now really? So, you've got something of Gerry's, but not your own sewing machine? Tell me more."

"It's in envelopes that were found in his office. I had a look. There are gas receipts, and I think the fish plant road was more expensive than it had to be." There was silence at the other end of the phone.

"Listen. Aren't you busy with some kind of craft deal? Why don't you stick to that? Gerry's death is not any of your business. But if you've got papers you want us to have, drop them off at the station. Leave them at the front desk."

"Will you look at them?"

"Sure, sure, I will." Wade attempted a professionally soothing tone. "And good luck with finding your sewing machine. It'll turn up."

⌒⌒

Frustrated, I stared at my phone. I was giving up on adult humans. If no one else would talk to me, at least I knew Toby would listen, so I went home. As I climbed the three front steps to my aunt's bungalow, I heard the big retriever's tail slapping back and forth on the walls of the tiny entry. Is there any better feeling in the world than coming home to a dog? I didn't think there was.

I often felt Toby was sent to me, right at the moment I knew I wasn't meant to live alone. It had happened in early winter, just after I'd come back to Gasper's. I was teaching one of my first evening sewing classes and we were on break, my students out in the store getting tea from the big urn Rollie had set up for us, when Sarah Chisholm came charging in, letting in all the cold air from outside. Breathlessly, she told us about an abandoned dog, left in front of the animal shelter, a rope tied between his collar and the handle of the front door. The dog, although well fed and cared for, was shivering and confused. A shelter volunteer had been called at home and arrived in minutes, indignantly complaining of tourists who brought animals on vacation and then found them too much work. The dog had been brought inside, and there he still waited, for a family who had long driven away.

Zippers didn't matter that night, and I ended class early. When I got to the shelter, a massive golden retriever with hope in his large brown eyes was waiting for me. I called him Toby, after my dad's first dog, and we'd been together ever since.

Toby sensed my feelings, and I knew his. So, when I got home, we looked at each other and decided that after the intensity of the last few days, we both needed a long walk. I put on Toby's leash, and we went down to Front Street, past the boats at the wharf, and onto the paths that led through the hills out of town. Once the roads were behind us, I let Toby free. He bounded off, zigzagging over rocks, lichen, and grass, nose to the ground, following the smells of the earth and of life, long buried by winter and released by spring.

I loved this little island, so close to the mainland that it almost, but not quite, touched it. I sometimes wondered what brought our ancestors here, to this exact spot, save for the fact that these rocks, these hills, and this ocean reminded them of the coast of Scotland they'd left behind. Perhaps they had felt less homesick here.

How had they ever survived? My dad told me once that the original Rankins had spent their first months not far from where I was now, the whole family sheltered under an overturned boat, the side supported by bales of hay. Who would do that now, in the bitter, wet winters we still had? But they did it, no doubt driven by memories of the starvation the Highlanders faced at home, but perhaps just as motivated by an understanding that this hard, beautiful place would not let down people like itself.

And they had built something, left something for us. I turned and looked back at the town wrapped around the cove, tight and secure, the modest wood frame houses so neatly kept, the fishing boats so securely tied up at the wharf. This was what I had come back for. A solid place where things lasted, where the generations flowed into each other, determination, humor, and family bonds passed down, hand to hand. I settled into myself. I sat down on a large, round granite rock and watched my dog's joy, looked out over the water, and thought about nothing at all until it was time to go back.

When I called Toby, he came to me, twigs from his adventures caught in his blond fur, foam along the loose sides of his doggy lips, panting and happy. We turned back the way we had come and walked down into the town. The light was thinner now. It was getting late, and so instead of walking back along the boardwalk, we took the shortcut down the back lane, behind the buildings. This route took us past the United Church.

We were almost there when I saw two familiar figures walk across the parking lot to several parked cars.

Two councilors. Harry Sutherland and Darlene's uncle Frank.

Instinctively, I pulled Toby back behind a large recycling bin. What were they doing here so late and together? Frank had been a pastor once, but this wasn't his church. It didn't make sense. I held my dog still and retreated further into the shadows. In twice as many days, Harry had intruded into my life. Was this a coincidence? The two reached their cars and drove off. I stood and watched them go and then bent down to my dog.

"Mr. Toby, enough is enough. Time to go see your Auntie Darlene." At her name, the dog wagged his tail. We crossed the street, and instead of stopping at home, headed up the hill to my cousin's house and, I hoped, some answers.

CHAPTER SIXTEEN

Darlene lived at the end of a cul-de-sac called Flying Cloud Drive. I always wondered what burst of whimsy at the planning office had inspired the name but was happy to think even bureaucrats were romantic.

Her house was much like my aunt's bungalow, with the addition of a side porch with a door down to the salon. I envied the life Darlene had made for herself. Even though men came and went, Darlene had stayed here, always the same, her cash flow and rhythm uninterrupted.

There were lights on in the basement—Darlene had a late client. I took Toby up to the kitchen and went down to the salon.

It was glamorous down there. The salon's color scheme was modern and chic—white walls and black decor, with a gilt Greek key border that ran along the top of the walls, dipping up, down, and around the small basement windows. Darlene had done all the painting and stenciling herself and was very proud of her cursive work behind the appointment desk. "If you're happy, I'm happy" it read. Three of the salon's walls were covered in framed trade posters collected at the industry training sessions Darlene never missed, each intended to inspire hair colors and styles unlikely to ever be worn in Gasper's Cove. The remaining wall, the one behind the sinks, was reserved for Darlene's certificates and diplomas: Master Stylist, Advanced Colorist, Spa Management.

This evening Darlene was at the sinks. Maureen McRae, Mack's wife, was in the chair, her head tilted back, water running down her brown, wavy hair, her glasses held tight in the manicured hands folded over the plastic cape. Darlene heard me come down the stairs, paused to give me a short smile, and then continued her conversation with Maureen.

"Sure, I'll donate. Now, which committee is this for?" Darlene asked as she worked conditioner into Maureen's dripping hair.

"The Beach Cleanup, not the Ladies Golf Association, the auxiliary, or the church. This is the last year I will be chairing the cleanup. There's some bylaw about not being chair more than three times in a row, but I can't imagine who else would do it. So much work."

"Got it. You're a busy lady. What would we all do without you?" Darlene was distracted. "Excuse me, Mrs. McRae. I'll be a moment." She wiped her hands and walked over to me.

"We have to talk," I whispered. "I left a bunch of messages."

"I know. I know. I got them. I'm really busy. Look around— still at it."

"I don't want to bug you at work. I'm going upstairs. Toby and I can wait until you're free. Okay?"

"Are we done at the sink?" Maureen called. "I have to get ready for Meals on Wheels early tomorrow morning. I promised the board. There's no one else to do it."

"I'm coming," Darlene said, then turned to me, her face carefully blank. "I'll be up there in a bit."

Up the narrow stairs again, I joined Toby in Darlene's small, impossibly neat kitchen, and sat down to wait. Cuddles, Darlene's large orange cat, glared at me and jumped up on the counter to watch with disdain as the dog finished the last of her supper.

"Sorry, Cuddles. I had to bring him. I need to see your mom." Unimpressed, the cat stood, jumped down onto the floor, and stalked past me and out of the room, tail erect. No one in this household, it seemed, was happy to see me.

After a while, I heard the crunch of gravel as Maureen's car left the driveway. Shortly afterward Darlene bustled up the stairs.

"What is it that can't wait? It's been a long day," she asked, stopping to pat Toby before she turned to lower the dishwasher door.

I might as well get right to it.

"I need to talk to you. I know you picked up Harry at the casino the other night. Someone saw you. It doesn't matter who. But I want to know. What's going on?"

Silence.

Darlene reached down and picked up a clean glass. She turned her back to me and opened a cupboard door. "Nothing's going on. Just a friend helping a friend."

She'd have to do better than that. "Since when were you and Harry friends? Come on."

Darlene reached for another glass.

"Listen, Valerie ..." She never called me Valerie. "This isn't something I can discuss with you. And to be honest, it's none of your business."

I stared at her. Darlene's business had been my business for as long as I remembered. "Are you kidding me? You're like this about Harry?"

"You ask too many questions. Anyone ever tell you that?"

"All the time. That's beside the point. Off-topic." I wasn't giving up. This wasn't like Darlene. Toby worked his way to the bottom of the water bowl. Cuddles returned to the kitchen, arched her back, and stared at him, her eyes round and unblinking.

Darlene stood and pushed the top rack of the dishwasher back. She'd left two glasses in the dishwasher. Wine glasses.

Then it hit me. "Don't tell me you are getting serious about Brent?" I had an image of Brent and Harry, side by side at the council meeting.

Darlene crossed her arms over her chest. "If I was, would it be such a bad thing?" she asked.

"Come on. We used to laugh at what a sleaze he was in high school. Don't you remember?"

"We're not in high school anymore. That's the point. He's changed, and he needs me."

I rolled my eyes. "Here we go again. All men aren't like your brothers; you don't need to take care of them." Darlene had been the only girl, and the oldest, with seven younger brothers. Her mother always used to tell anyone who'd listen that she didn't know what she'd do without her Darlene. Taking care of males was a hard habit to break. "I don't know why, but Brent's using you. He's got you running around for him, doing errands and who knows what."

"Don't start with that again. This is completely different, and you don't know what you're talking about." Darlene's words were clipped as she slapped a sponge down onto a spotless counter and started wiping.

"Oh, I think I do," I said. "It's always the same. These guys just see the boobs and the hair, and they completely miss what matters about you." I didn't have it in me to watch Darlene be let down again. I didn't.

She laughed, but not because there was anything funny. "What else is there?"

"Lots. When that liar I married left, you didn't say, 'I told you so,' like everyone else. You got in the car and drove to the city with your crochet, your housecoat, and a bottle of rosé. You sat up with me once the kids were in bed and listened to me say the same things over and over again. I'll never forget it. You don't let people down. Not ever."

Darlene put down her sponge and came over and sat down at the kitchen table with me. "That was a bad time, Val, but you know what? It's over. We can't spend our whole lives talking about what was unfair or what we did wrong. I need my turn. I'm ready to move on."

Move on? Did she mean without me? I didn't know what she was talking about. But I knew it was important. So I acted like I got it.

"I understand," I said, which was a lie. "But promise me you know who you're getting involved with. Gerry knew something was wrong at the council—little things, maybe big things. Now he's dead."

Darlene pushed back her chair, picked up the milk jug from the table, and put it in the fridge, slamming the door so hard that some of her souvenir magnets fell off and rolled across the floor. "Are you telling me you think Brent had something to do with what happened to Gerry? You cannot be serious."

I'd crossed a line, but I didn't regret it. "I'm not saying that. I don't know what's going on. It's stressing me out. I don't trust Brent. Why don't you tell me why you went and got Harry? It's a simple question. I don't know why you're so mad at me." I knew I sounded desperate, but I was.

Darlene glanced at down Toby and Cuddles and struggled to speak calmly. The atmosphere in the room was upsetting the two animals.

"What I told you about Harry is the truth. I was just helping out a friend. You have to believe it." She picked up her fluffy cat and held her close. "You're wrong about Brent. He's not like the other guys. I know what they saw in me. I'm not stupid. Everyone thinks I am, but I'm not. You know what Brent says about me?"

I shook my head; I could only imagine.

"Brent tells me I have good ideas, that I am smart." Darlene gave me a hard look like I'd let her down. "I've waited a long time to hear that from someone." She looked at the big clock on the wall above the stove. "It's late. You should go."

There was nothing left for me to do or to say. So, I stood and clipped Toby's leash to his collar, and we left. Walking down Darlene's driveway and out to the rest of Flying Cloud Drive, my chest hurt, and my legs felt stiff as my feet slapped flatly on the asphalt. I needed to fix this. Maybe I should go back. I stopped and turned to look back at Darlene's house.

There was no one at the window. The kitchen light went out.

CHAPTER SEVENTEEN

As Toby and I walked home, I retreated to thinking about my sewing classes, an anchor in my life. I could do those right. Summer term. My students would love swimwear. Everyone would expect bathing suits to be hard, but they weren't. I had most of what I needed for this class at home: lots of nice fabric and some good basic patterns. But what about a sewing machine? I'd need one for topstitching and elastic application, even if many of the students used sergers for the structural seams. But my classroom machine was gone, stolen, even if no one else believed it. I'd have to take my aunt's old Singer into the store until I figured out what to do next.

Back at the house, I filled Toby's bowl and then grabbed Gerry's two envelopes off the dining room table. I'd do exactly what Wade said and drop off the documents with the RCMP. This was a real murder investigation; time for Noah and me to let it go.

But I couldn't face Wade on an empty stomach. I opened the fridge door and took out a covered bowl of casserole.

How old was it? I lifted the plate on top and sniffed. It would be fine; I'd made it two days ago, although that seemed a lifetime away, so much had happened. I needed tea. I opened the cupboard beside the sink, took out a big cup and a tea bag, and reached for the electric kettle to fill it. At the sink, I paused. The kettle was already almost full and still warm. When had I turned the kettle on? I unplugged it. I better get a new one. Last thing I needed was to electrocute myself.

I sat at the kitchen table and drank tea made from water heated in the microwave. When I finished eating, I put my dishes in the sink; I'd load the dishwasher later. I turned on the light to the basement and went down. My aunt's old machine was basic. I'd put in a twin needle and show the students how to do a stretchy topstitch. They'd like that.

At the bottom of the stairs, I noticed a flicker deep in the dark. What was it? I reached over and turned on the switch for the large fluorescent lights in the tiled ceiling. The old lights blinked for a moment and then flooded the basement with light.

I took a step toward my aunt's sewing alcove and stopped. The sewing cabinet was open, and the ancient Singer levitated to its upright position. I was sure I hadn't left it up, but this wasn't what caught my attention.

Right beside the Singer, to the left, on the cabinet's extension table, was my missing sewing machine. The same machine that had gone to the hospital and was then taken from the trunk of my car as it sat in the driveway. Here it was, formerly stolen and now returned, brought back to my house by anonymous hands.

My legs shook as I walked over to the machines. I sat on the little stool with its hidden thread storage space under the cushion. I stared at the missing, now found, machine. If only it could talk. Where had it been? I looked closer. The machine was plugged in and ready to sew. The blood on the throat plate was gone, and a new needle had been installed. It was a universal, put in properly with the flat part of the shaft to the back, something many people got wrong. The machine had been threaded, too, and the bobbin thread pulled up. I checked the bobbin. It was full, newly wound. Shocking pink. My favorite color.

I went still. Whoever had taken the machine had come into my house and returned it. They were in control, and worse, they knew me, and knew me well.

⌒⌒⌒

I ran upstairs as if chased by the ghost of sewing machines past. I grabbed my purse, pushed past Toby, ran down the front steps, and jumped in my car. The old Toyota and I flew across the causeway to the RCMP office. When I arrived, I knew I was in luck. Two marked vehicles were in the lot. Hopefully, both Wade and Nolan would be in. They should both hear this.

The officer at the front desk didn't share my urgency.

"They're pretty busy in here today," she said from her seat behind the plexiglass divider. "What's this about?"

"Tell them I have information pertinent to the murder investigation," I said, assuming that only one murder had been committed recently in the greater Gasper's Cove–Drummond area.

The desk officer was unimpressed, and she sat for a moment trying to decide what to do with me. "I'll buzz them," she said. "Please take a seat."

115

It was a long wait for a woman who had recently discovered stolen merchandise in her aunt's basement, but I sat. Eventually, Officer Nolan came out to see me.

"Hi there, Ms. Rankin. Why don't you come in and tell us what you have to say? We have a few minutes."

I was surprised by her indifference. Is this how the RCMP caught criminals?

Wade remained seated when I entered the office. Nolan motioned me to a chair in front of the desk but remained standing near the door as if trying to decide if she should stay or leave.

It was time I was taken seriously. "First thing first," I said. "Gerry was murdered, wasn't he?"

Nolan's voice behind me was curt. "This is now a homicide investigation, yes."

"Good thing I came in then," I said to them both. "I have information you're going to want to see."

Wade made a steeple with his fingers in front of his face and stared at me. I had the impression this was a move he had seen on some cop show.

"Is this about some papers of Gerry's you say you had?" he asked me. "I told you to leave them at the desk."

Ignoring him, I unloaded some knitting and a few small plastic bags for dog walking onto his desk and threw down Gerry's envelopes. "Anything this important I decided to hand deliver," I said, expecting that this would give me the full attention of both officers.

Wade picked up the envelopes and dropped them into a wire basket marked "Out."

I was outraged but kept going. "That's not all," I said. "Remember the sewing machine that was stolen?"

"I remember some story about a sewing machine. What about it?"

"I have a new crime to report," I said.

Wade looked at Nolan, but she was staring at the ceiling.

"What?" Wade asked. "What else have you lost?"

"Nothing. That's the crime. The sewing machine is back. It's in my basement."

"Right."

Dawn Nolan stepped forward and leaned down to me, speaking to me in the soft voice you would use with a child. "Valerie, people usually don't report things they find in their own homes."

I was getting annoyed. These two weren't behaving professionally. Now it was my turn to talk slowly. "No, you aren't getting it. Someone stole my sewing machine because they knew it would scare me. Then they snuck into my house and returned it to freak me out even more." I looked back and forth between the two officers. "Which it did. This was a warning to me, personally. A message. They want me to back off and be quiet because they think I know what Gerry knew. But I don't. It's all there." I pointed to the envelopes. My voice was getting shrill, but I didn't care. "Put them in the 'In' basket, Wade. Read it all. Have a good look at the notes on the cereal box."

"Cereal box?" Nolan asked and took a step back.

"Yes. Cap'n Crunch."

Wade pushed his chair away from his desk. "Right. Okay, Valerie. Thanks for coming in. You bring a car? Do you think you are okay with driving home?" He and Nolan exchanged a look. "I can have someone drive you."

"No, no. I'm fine." It was my turn to stand. "Look at the envelopes, the gas receipts, the expense reports. You'll see what I mean. And ..." I continued, then paused, with what I hoped was a flourish of dignity and confidence, "I'll find out who returned my sewing machine myself."

"You do that," Wade said. "Let us know how it works out."

I thought I heard laughter behind me as I pushed open the glass door of the building on my way out, but maybe I was wrong. One thing I was sure of. I was on my own.

Before I pulled away from the RCMP building I decided I needed to call Noah. I had turned Gerry's files over without asking him first, and I felt guilty. I was treating him like a kid, like my kid, and that had to stop. But I did what I had to because I was afraid. Someone had been in my house, tried to frighten me, and it had worked.

He answered on the first ring.

"I have to tell you something. I handed the stuff you gave me over to the RCMP."

"You did what? Without asking me? I don't get it."

"Something happened. I panicked. I got scared. I just did it."

Silence.

"Noah, where are you now?"

"At the library. Doing some research."

"I'll meet you there. I'll explain."

"I guess. I'll wait." He hung up.

When I got to the library, it took me some time to find Noah. He was off in a carrel at the far end of the reading room, out of sight, deep in documents. I could see why he was back there. Catherine was loading old yearbooks onto a table in the middle reading room and not doing it quietly. I pulled up a chair and sat close to the young reporter.

"Listen. I had to turn those files over to the police. This is murder, more than you and I should be handling on our own." Noah was annoyed but too well-mannered to ignore me. "Besides, something strange happened." I told him about the machine being taken, then returned, by someone who had come into my house. My story sounded peculiar even to me. Noah, at least, took me more seriously than Wade and Nolan had.

"That's creepy. You figure maybe someone on the council is trying to scare you off?"

"That's pretty much it. Getting paid twice for gas is crooked, but not horrendous. There has to be something else. Maybe this road thing ... I don't get it."

"What did this Stuart guy say?" Noah pulled a notebook and pen out of his backpack. I felt like I was being interviewed.

"He didn't say much. He was very careful and professional, but he said where they put the road meant they had to use more fill, whatever that means."

"Got it. My dad worked for the Department of Transportation. Fill is the rocks and soil they haul in to bring a surface up to grade. This is great. This is a lead." I was forgiven.

"So, who owns the fill?" With beams and dirt, I was getting more engineering information than I wanted, but not quite enough of engineers, I realized.

"Anyone with land, a quarry, and a truck, I guess. Who would that be?"

Our eyes locked.

Mack McRae.

Before he'd been a warden, he'd had a small construction company.

"But wouldn't that have disqualified him from municipal work?" I asked. I didn't have a clue how these things worked.

"In a small town, not necessarily," Noah said. "He wouldn't have had the road contract; he'd just end up as a subcontractor for the fill. He'd be a couple of layers down below scrutiny. And you've got to think of two things. First, no one on council would think to ask about the mechanics of something like fill. If they thought the road was necessary and saw trucks, they'd think it was normal. That's one thing. The second is these small councils have run without oversight forever. Why do you think the province decided to do audits?"

The Union of Nova Scotia Municipalities meetings. I remembered those now.

"It's all coming together." Noah was triumphant. "Harry was ripping off the town with his expenses. He gave Mack the lead about the road, which helped Mack divert business to his construction company. Gerry had it all figured out and was probably going to tip off the auditors and get the story, and now Gerry is dead."

"Are you saying what I think you are?"

"Yes, I am. The good old warden is a killer."

CHAPTER EIGHTEEN

"Now what?" Noah asked me.

I held up my phone and I headed to the library's front door. This was a call to make outside, in private. I dialed the number of the RCMP detachment I had just left.

The plexiglass officer picked up immediately. "Both Officers Corkum and Nolan are out on a call. Can I give them a message?"

I hesitated. "I'd like to speak to one of them in person. Can I leave a number? Can you get in touch with them? It's life-and-death important."

"I'm sure it is, Ms. Rankin. They'll get back to you at the next available opportunity. I promise."

What could I do? "Please tell them I called. It's urgent."

"Will do." She hung up.

I went back into the library to report to Noah. He had left his carrel and was sitting with Catherine, leafing through old yearbooks.

"I don't believe this. There are so many of them here—not in the same year, of course, but they all went to high school together. Look at this," he said, raising his eyebrows and pointing at the picture of the graduating class of 1982. There was Mack, front and center, laughing with the confidence of the handsome prince he was.

"Did you make the call? What did they say?"

I sat close to him and waited until Catherine got up to help a library patron. "They'll get back to me."

"What do we do? Wait? When we know a murderer is running around?"

I scanned the library for listeners. "Lower your voice. No one knows we know. Let's keep it that way. They'll call me; then they'll pick him up ..." I hesitated. "That's what they do, right? Pick him up?"

"Guess. Seems weird, particularly when you see this." He pointed at the yearbook open in front of him.

The *Garnet and Gold*. I'd forgotten. Darlene and I had gone to this high school ourselves, but later. Leafing through, I picked out Linda. *The queen of the chess club, the debating club, and, no wait, can this be true? The football fan club? Someone melted the snow queen's heart, and we all know who.* Kenny MacQuarrie, aviator glasses and greasy bangs, a couple of years ahead of Mack, nothing written beside his name. Maureen Cameron, *She came, she conquered, and she'll have fun, fun, fun till her daddy takes the Mustang away,* and, of course, Mack himself, *Is there anything this all-star jock can't do? Biology? Math? Hey, Mr. Clarke, I was at practice. Good thing his queen is such a brainiac.*

I stared at the faces. The men all had less hair now, and the women a few more pounds, but I recognized the earlier editions of Mack, Kenny, Linda, and Maureen (then Cameron, now McRae). These were hints of life stories. Linda and

Mack were an item in high school, but at some point, he'd moved on to Maureen. Had he dumped her in high school, and she'd resented him ever since? I shook my head. It was a long time to nurse a grudge. A long time.

Noah was fixed on the picture of the young Mack. "This kid grew up and became a killer. That's not in the yearbook. I think I'll go home and start writing the story. What are you going to do?"

"Wait too, I guess." Linda hadn't gotten back to me about Gerry's microfiche. I had a copy of the map, so it didn't matter, but it didn't seem like her not to have called me as promised. "Something else I have to do while I'm here. Don't worry. When the police call, you'll be the first to know."

Noah hoisted his backpack onto a shoulder and headed to the library's exit. I got up and went off in search of Linda.

Her office was easy to locate—near the back, next to a two-level water fountain, with a step stool set up for junior patrons. The door was closed. I knocked.

"Come in."

Linda sat behind her desk but had swiveled her chair so it faced the window. She turned, her face white, her eyes in shock.

"I'm sorry—am I bothering you?"

Linda sniffed. "What do you want?"

"I thought I'd let you know Catherine helped me with the microfiche business of Gerry's. I have a copy of the map, so you can forget about it."

"Oh. Good." She stared at me as if willing me to leave. "Anything else?"

"No, thanks." All the detail in those envelopes probably didn't matter now; the identity of Gerry's killer was clear, but I had to admit I was still curious. How deep had the corruption on the council gone? My hunter's instinct, now released, was reluctant to retreat.

I hesitated. Linda's office didn't look as if anyone worked there. The desk was clear. There were no framed pictures, no potted plants, no silly mug with "Librarians do it between the covers" on it. It was a lonely person's workplace, and somehow more so today.

"Linda, are you all right?"

She sniffed and pulled a ball of tissues from the sleeve of her cardigan. "You haven't heard?"

"No, what?"

"My sister's boy works at the yacht club. RCMP is there now. It's Mack. Maureen says she left him on the boat, but he never came in. He's gone." She blew her nose.

"What do you mean by gone?"

"The pair of them were on the boat last night and had supper on it. Maureen came into shore to go home and let the dog out. My nephew brought her in with the Zodiac. Mack stayed, said he wanted to have one more beer, watch the sun go down, come in later."

I tried to shift my mind. This was my murderer, relaxing on his boat.

Linda continued, "When he didn't show up at home, Maureen waited until morning, then went back out to check on him."

"Then what happened?" I couldn't rush the librarian as much as I wanted to.

"The boat was empty. A couple of bottles on the table, his cell phone, keys. But no Mack. Not a trace."

"So they think he fell off the boat?" Something wasn't right about this story.

Linda sniffed again. "They are doing search and rescue in the harbor right now. Man overboard. Officers Corkum and Nolan are at the club now. The Mounties are sending over more officers from Drummond. Mack was the warden, and that makes it an even bigger deal."

My mind whirled. No wonder Wade and Nolan hadn't called me back. They'd been dealing with this.

Then my thoughts skidded to a stop. This didn't mean Mack hadn't murdered Gerry. If Noah and I had figured everything out, it was only a matter of time until the police did, too. The walls were closing in. There was no way out for the warden.

Unless he disappeared.

CHAPTER NINETEEN

The search for Mack McRae continued over the weekend. With every hour, I became more and more convinced Mack was a killer who'd staged his own disappearance. I kept calling the RCMP office to leave messages. Eventually, Dawn Nolan turned up on my doorstep.

She strode into my living room in heavy boots.

"This has to stop."

"Excuse me. I gave you evidence. Mack was crooked; he killed Gerry."

"I don't know what you are talking about." Nolan was tired. "I like you, but you need to know. You're getting a reputation down at the station."

"A reputation? For what?"

"As a public nuisance. These stories are getting crazier and crazier. The sewing machines, the envelopes with secret papers inside. We don't have energy for this. You're lucky I even came out to talk to you."

"The receipts, the expense reports, the map? Didn't you see them? It's right there."

"Right where? All there was in those envelopes were Gerry's shopping lists. He needed socks. No receipts, nothing of interest."

"What? Look again." Nolan rolled her eyes sideways. She didn't think I'd caught it, but I had. "What about the back of the cereal box? Didn't that tell you something?"

"All it told us was Gerry liked Cap'n Crunch." Nolan spread her stance and put her hands on her hips. Even in her padded vest with "Police" on the front, she looked like a mother about to ground a bad kid. "Enough. No more." She turned and headed for the door.

"Wait," I called after her. "Mack's escaping."

Nolan stopped and turned slowly, very slowly, and stared at me. "Weren't you listening? Don't you ever tell me how to do my job. You have no idea what you're talking about."

"What do you mean?"

"We found Mack McRae."

"Good. Where'd you pick him up? The airport?"

"No."

"The ferry?"

"No."

"The border?"

"No, in the water. Tide brought him in. Forensics says foul play." Nolan stared up at the stippled plaster ceiling of the living room. "We have a job to do, and the last thing we need is to divert resources following up hysterical fantasies. Is this clear?"

I nodded and stood aside as she stalked out, slamming the door so hard the figurines in the china cabinet rattled.

⌒⊙⌒

After Officer Nolan left, I lay on the floor. I felt so low, this seemed like the best place for me. Toby lay beside me and let me rest my head on him, a massive, breathing, furry pillow of sympathy and solidarity. I lay with him for a long time, my tears of humiliation falling onto his back until finally the big dog shifted and licked them off my face with his wet, rough tongue.

I'd been so sure I'd figured it all out. I'd tied it up neatly— the financial scams at the council, Mack, an explanation for Gerry's death. What I'd done, I realized, was to try to find a reason for the unexplainable, to make my little world sane and safe again. I'd been wrong. About everything.

Toby and I would have lain there forever, or at least until supper, if there hadn't been a knock at the front door. I rolled off the dog, onto my knees, and then dragged myself to the front door, wiping tears off my face with my sleeve as I went.

There, on my front steps, was Stuart Campbell.

He took a step back. "Catch you at a bad moment?"

"Mack's been murdered," I said, as if this explained everything.

"I heard. I'm sorry. I didn't know you were close."

"It's not that. We weren't. I hardly knew him. It's complicated."

For an awkward beat, Stuart stared at me. "Okay ..." He held up a bag. "Friendship bracelets. Erin's been working on them. Her own designs, but I helped her do them on AutoCAD. I told her I'd drop them over."

I took the bag. "Thank her for me." He was a good father. I stood there at the open door.

"Listen," Stuart said carefully. "I feel kind of bad showing up like this when you're upset. Is there anything I can do? Maybe we can talk about it?"

"Really? Would you mind?" I asked. There was something about this man, even just standing there on the front steps, that made me feel calm. "Do you want to come in?"

Stuart hesitated for a moment, then decided. "Erin's at a friend's. I've got time. Sure." Once in the living room, Stuart did a slow circuit, taking in the hundreds of salt and pepper shakers, the pole lamp, the smocked cushions on the couch, and the glass grapes in a bowl. He let out a soft whistle.

"Whoa! This all yours?"

I looked around the room and saw it with his eyes. What was a woman my age doing living by herself in a mid-century time warp?

"It's my aunt's house. She's moved to Florida. I'm house-sitting. Not sure if she's ever coming back. In the meantime, it's me, my dog"—I gestured to Toby, who was dancing around Stuart as if he were some long-lost relative—"and a houseful of ornaments."

"I see." Stuart bent over and carefully picked up a granny square afghan from the floor. He folded it, put it neatly on the couch, and then sat beside it. "You were in Halifax, weren't you?"

"Right. Me and the kids until they moved away," I said. "One day, I realized I didn't want to spend the rest of my life in the place they'd left. It would be like living surrounded by empty spaces." As I listened to my own words, I realized this was true. I'd never put it together before.

"I get it," Stuart said. I realized he did.

I had a thought. "Have you eaten? It's just leftovers but I have ham and scalloped potatoes." I felt vulnerable and foolish, but I didn't want him to leave.

"Are you sure? I have never in my life turned down ham and scalloped potatoes. Just ask my mother." He stood. "Anything I can do to help you?"

And he did help. Reaching up high into my aunt's dusty collection of liquor bottles over the fridge, Stuart found an old bottle of merlot and opened it for us. I fed Toby first; then we helped ourselves to the ham and potatoes, heated our plates in the microwave, and sat at the dining room table.

It had been a while since I'd had anyone for dinner, but somehow, Stuart didn't seem like company. He complimented me on the food and poured me a second glass of wine, and I relaxed.

"So why don't you tell me why you were so upset when I got here," he asked. "What's going on? Is it about what happened to Mack?"

I put down my fork. "I've made a fool of myself with the police. If I tell you everything, would you promise to tell me, honestly, if you think I am completely crazy?"

"I promise." Stuart was solemn. "I absolutely will tell you if I think you are nuts. I know nuts."

"All right. Here goes." I told him everything: Gerry, the scandal he'd hinted at, Noah, the envelopes, the trip to the casino, and even the machine stolen and returned, as unhinged as that last part sounded.

When I finished, Stuart said nothing. He stared at the crochet tablecloth and reached down to pat Toby, who was stationed under the table, close to the food.

While I waited for him to say something, I carried the dishes to the kitchen, made tea, and brought it back to the table.

Stuart straightened in his chair. "This is what I think. And I have a few questions."

"Go ahead. I'm ready."

"First, I don't think you're crazy." He held up his hand and counted off the reasons on his fingers. "Here's why. Number one. I think Noah might be right. Gerry's murder didn't come out of nowhere. I agree Gerry might have discovered something, even more than we know." Finger number two went up. "Stopping an investigation is a powerful motivation for killing any reporter. Number three. Some financial irregularities were going on with the council. The police say they didn't find anything significant in the envelopes, but that doesn't mean it hadn't been there. You're forgetting you showed me those survey maps. They were real." His ring finger went up. "Number four. This business about the machine—okay, it's crazy, but crazy enough to be true. Someone's messing with your head. And as I already told you, I can spot a maniac, and you're not one. I mean, my kid's making you friendship bracelets."

"Thanks, but how do you explain it all? Everything pointed to Mack, and now he's dead."

"Not sure," Stuart admitted, "but there have been two deaths. Logically, we have to look at this from the killer's perspective." Stuart stirred milk into his tea. "Right now, we're looking at what we don't know. But what about what the killer doesn't know?"

"Excuse me?"

"Okay. Obviously, Gerry was a threat to the killer, but potentially, so are you. The killer doesn't know if Gerry told you anything. That uncertainty makes you an open risk. But he can't be sure. But killing someone else would attract attention. So, what would he do instead?"

"No idea." Stuart's clinical assessment of my safety was unnerving.

"Discredit you. If the killer can make it look like you are a wacko, then whatever you say, the police won't believe you. I also think there is a secondary reason for scaring you."

"A secondary reason? This is getting worse."

"The documents." Stuart was excited; he enjoyed puzzles. "We both saw them, or at least I saw the survey map, but they weren't there when the police looked. Maybe whoever returned your machine to the basement stopped off here in the dining room first"—he rapped on the table, waking up Toby—"and removed the most damning papers and notes. But left the envelopes so you wouldn't know right away."

He lifted his mug and smiled at me over the rim. "Clever, to be honest."

It made sense.

But it was incomplete. My turn.

"This is all great on the why. But it still leaves us with the who. I thought Mack was responsible for Gerry's death, but even if he was, then who killed Mack? How many bad guys do we have around here? I don't see the connection."

"We need a paradigm shift." Stuart's mind was racing, slotting information into some spreadsheet only he saw.

"A paradigm what?"

"A frame of reference. Assumptions." The ideas were assembling in his mind. "So far, it's looked like this was all about the council and internal expenses. But maybe it isn't. Maybe that's a false hypothesis, based on an incidental finding. It's possible Gerry and Mack were killed for some other reason entirely." Stuart sat back, pleased with himself. "How about that?"

"You've got to give me a moment on this. What are you saying?"

Stuart folded his napkin and laid his teaspoon neatly on it. "We don't know what information the police have; there has to be more to this. We need to trust them to take care of this."

"But what am I supposed to do?" I was now more confused than when we'd sat to eat.

Stuart was suddenly serious. "What you do is absolutely nothing. For some reason beyond me, you think you've established yourself as a ditz. So okay. The more flaky, unreliable, and harmless you seem, the safer, the less threatening you'll be."

Stuart stood and picked up his keys from the table. "I've got to pick up Erin now. But there is something I want you to do for me."

"What's that?" I asked as we walked to the door together.

"I want you to make sure you lock your doors, and if anything happens, call the police, and call me, too. I mean it." He hesitated, then reached out as if to give me a one-armed hug. Sensing the emotion, Toby moved between us, tail wagging, pushing us apart.

Stuart laughed and reached down to pat Toby instead.

"Keep her safe," he said to the big dog. Then he was gone.

I went to the living room window and watched Stuart drive away. The house was suddenly empty. I turned off the lights and went into the kitchen to clean up before I went to bed. With just me in the house, I only ran the dishwasher every few days, and it was overdue.

"Toby, my man, what do you think of that one?" I asked the big dog. Toby slapped his tail on the linoleum tiles, pleased to be asked his opinion.

I opened the dishwasher door. As I pulled out the top rack, I remembered the two wine glasses I'd seen at Darlene's. Had I been unfair to her about Brent Cameron?

My hand froze.

There at the very back of my dishwasher was a single teacup—a good one, my grandmother's, bone china, one that had to be hand washed. I hadn't put it there; I never would. I looked through the kitchen door to the tall china cabinet in the dining room. I could see a lone saucer, out of place, at the front of the third shelf.

I remembered the warm kettle I had touched just before I had discovered the returned machine. My chest constricted. I couldn't breathe. Someone had come into my house, taken Gerry's papers, put the machine in the basement, and made themselves a cup of tea.

I wasn't safe. Not at all.

CHAPTER TWENTY

If someone was deliberately trying to unnerve me, they had succeeded. I spent the whole night afraid, a seam ripper under my pillow, my phone on the bedside table, wondering if whoever had entered my house once would return. From my bed, I looked down the bungalow's hallway to the living room, my eyes searching the dark for menacing shapes, my ears straining for unexpected sounds. But as alert as I was, all I saw were the shadows from the streetlamp outside, and all I heard were the snores of my guard dog, blissfully asleep on the bed beside me.

By morning, I knew I couldn't do this anymore. Being scared made me angry, and indignation flowed up through me, across my shoulders, and down my arms. I looked down at my hands and was surprised to see them clenched into fists.

"Toby. What's happening to your mom? Enough. We're smart. Get up, my boy. Let's make a plan."

Relaxed, the big dog rolled over onto his back and beamed at me, big brown eyes full of trust and patience. However, sensing my resolve, and no doubt ready for breakfast, he jumped off the bed and joined me on my trek down to my aunt's pink and gray bathroom.

I turned on the light and looked at the sink. There was one toothbrush in the cup. For so many years there had been four. My three children were coming back at the end of the summer, to catch up with each other and, I knew, to see how I was doing. I wanted them to be proud of me. I stared at the ceramic flamingos on the wall, and I assessed my situation. Before I could do anything else I needed to know where I was safe and where I wasn't. Right now, I felt the unknown was stalking me. I had to turn that around and put a face to it.

But where to start?

The largest question in my mind was the one closest to me. Who was watching me? This was the key. The machine was stolen because someone saw me put it in the trunk of my car in the hospital parking lot. Was this a coincidence, or had I been followed? I remembered the sensation of being observed when I was on Adelaide Street after my first meeting with Stuart. And even worse, someone had watched me at home, known when I'd gone out, and then waited for a chance to slip in. I thought of Gerry's envelopes. Who had passed this information on to him? Surely not the same person who had come into the house and taken it back. This didn't make sense. Were there two people involved? Was one trying to expose corruption on the council and one trying to protect it? If this was the case, which one was stalking me?

And what about Stuart?

His almost clinical assessment of the danger I was in unnerved me, but at the same time, I appreciated his interest. As a single mother I had been on my own a long, long time, and male company was not something I had the energy to indulge in. But as someone new to my life, Stuart had shown objectivity about my situation that Rollie and Darlene didn't have. He could have seen me the way Wade or Nolan did, and he was right—I had little credibility left with them. It wouldn't matter what I uncovered now; I'd be the last person they'd believe. But Stuart was only half right; establishing my unreliability didn't feel like the only reason someone would watch or harass me. There was something else.

The store. The development. That had to be it. Like many old-time general stores, Rankin's needed a new angle to survive. For us, becoming a craft-based tourist destination might work. But if the idea failed, or was stopped, Rankin's might yet be replaced by a shinier, more shallow business.

What had I said to Noah?

That the fraud in the council was a sign of larger corruption. Were the "progressives," Brent and Harry, mixed up with the developers? Had their support been bought? Had Mack, to date guilty mainly of hubris and fiscal indiscretion, been murdered because his vote on the heritage proposal stood in their way?

I needed more information. I sent off another email to Julie Chandler.

Hey, Julie. Wondering if you found out anything about this Lars Nyberg guy? Appreciate the help, Val.

I sat staring at my laptop and waited for an answer. When none came, I took Toby for a walk around the block and thought about my plan. Until I heard from Julie, I had other issues to investigate. And I knew who was at the top of the list.

Harry. He was clearly trouble. His gambling gave him a motive for theft, and his position on the council had given him the opportunity to do it. Strangely, he'd crossed my path a lot in the last few days—in the restaurant, at the council, outside the casino, and behind the church. Had he been in the hospital parking lot too? In my house? What was Darlene's real connection with him? And why was she hiding it?

My cousin and best friend and I had unfinished business. As Toby and I turned the corner to go back home, I pulled out my phone and tapped in her number.

> We need to talk. Lunch? Tomorrow?

I waited.

> Sorry about the other night. Can I count on your support?

This sounded a little odd, but an apology felt good.

> Of course, always. Noon?

> See you then.

CᏅᎧ

Darlene was at the restaurant when I arrived. I was reassured to see that our usual order was already on the table. Maybe things hadn't changed between us after all.

"Me first," Darlene said. "About the other night. I know I hurt your feelings, but you were pushing too hard. Not everything's your business. Let it go."

I suddenly realized that nothing made me want to hang on as much as someone telling me not to. I still wanted to know what was happening, and I had to figure out how to get Darlene to tell me.

Sensing I wasn't going to give up, Darlene tried to distract me with more current news. "Terrible about Mack. Do you believe it?"

"Not really. It's too crazy. How's Maureen doing?"

"She's devastated, but I give her credit. She's tough—she still came in to get her roots done on schedule." Darlene paused to think. "You know, it's funny. When I talked to her it was almost as if she was a little mad at Mack. Like what did he do to get himself murdered? It's as if he'd let her down. He was her whole world. I'm not sure what she'll do with herself now."

"Maureen's on every committee in town," I pointed out. "There's always that."

Darlene had finished eating. "That would not be enough for everyone," she said, carefully arranging her cutlery in the exact center of her plate and pouring herself another glass of water.

"What do you mean by that?" I asked, alert. I had known Darlene my whole life. I knew when she was circling in on news I might not like.

"Brent called me," she said. "He feels terrible. He knew Mack well. But this means the warden's position on the council is now open. It's too early to do anything, but ..." She hesitated. "You know how seriously Brent takes local government."

I wasn't sure I knew this at all, but I let it pass.

"He wants to make sure we have the right person to replace Mack." She leaned forward and lowered her voice. "Now this is just between us right now, but he's asked me if I would consider running for Mack's seat in the by-election."

"Whoa, whoa, Darlene," I said. "Do you hear yourself? This isn't like you. Someone's just died, and already your boyfriend's scheming. You okay with that?"

Darlene sat up straighter, pursing her mouth so only her lip liner showed.

"Excuse me. First, Brent is more a colleague than a boy-friend." I stared at her. I thought of her basement salon, and I thought of Brent's car dealership. Colleagues?

"Brent believes in my vision for the future."

"Darlene, this doesn't sound like you." Last week, all she wanted to talk about was why I needed lowlights. Now she had a vision. "Come on."

Darlene smacked down her glass, grabbed her purse, and glared at me.

"If this happened to Mack, it's because he was into some-thing bad. Who I feel for is Maureen, to tell the truth. It's terrible that he did this to her. But what happens next in the council is another story, nothing personal." Her eyes were wide, her eyelashes almost touching her auburn bangs. "What's wrong about talking about the future? Everyone around here thinks they can write the story of the rest of my life. Like I'm stalled, doomed never to change. Darlene. Nice person, good with hair, terrible at marriage, you should have seen her at 18."

She was not wrong; this was more or less what most people thought. But not me. I knew better. But did she know that? Had I told her?

Darlene was standing now, breathing hard. I caught George Kousolas's eye from across the restaurant. He looked concerned.

"And you know what's clear?" she asked, looking down at me. "There are two kinds of people in my life right now. Those who believe in me and think I can do something interesting with my life, and those who don't. The other night? Today? You've made it clear which one you are."

Slapping her portion of our lunch check down on the table hard, Darlene turned away. Then, the most talented hair stylist in eastern Nova Scotia, the godmother of my oldest child, and my best friend for as long as I remember walked out of the restaurant, leaving me behind.

CHAPTER TWENTY-ONE

After Darlene left, I did the only thing any reasonable person does when life gets messy. I ordered another dessert. If one piece of baklava, dripping with honey, couldn't fix this, two might.

I was scraping the last sticky crumbs from my plate when the door of the restaurant opened and in walked Lars Nyberg. I couldn't believe it. Here he was, the man whose arrival in Gasper's Cove had begun this cycle of upheaval and death, disrupting the peace I had expected to find here at home.

I opened my wallet and laid some bills on the money Darlene had left for our lunch and then signaled to George that I wanted another coffee and maybe a tiny third piece of baklava and pointed to the booth Nyberg now occupied. Like it or not, the mystery man now had a lunch companion.

I walked over to Nyberg. He looked up in surprise, not entirely glad to see me.

"Mind if I join you?" I asked, sitting before he could say no.

"Guess not. Valerie, isn't it?" Up close, Nyberg was like someone from an old black-and-white TV show—light-gray shirt, darker gray tie, black watch, black messenger bag on the seat beside him, black pants, black belt, and I knew if I checked under the table, black socks and shoes. His pale face and hair were grayed out too, like something you knew had color but was reduced to monotone by the television. Even his blue eyes seemed bleached out and faded behind the large, round black frames of his glasses.

"We need to talk," I said, nothing to lose. "I know you and the developer want to buy our store and demolish it. I've seen you with the councilors. I know what you're up to." No one would push me around.

Nyberg jerked his head back, offended. "Buy your store? What are you talking about? Who told you I have anything to do with a developer?"

"You were at the store the other day, weren't you? I saw your car out front. The very same day someone came in wanting us to sell."

"My car? You mean that one?" Nyberg turned his head to the street where a gray hybrid was parked. "Sure, I've been to your store. Nothing strange about that. I needed pencil leads." He picked up a mechanical pencil and held it up for me to see.

Had he switched cars? I was still suspicious. Who used pencils these days? And who would think Rankin's General Store carried those little, tiny leads? This guy was dodgy for sure.

"Then who are you? What are you doing here? Something's up."

Lars Nyberg eyed me with a combination of caution and annoyance. Eerily, this was the same expression I'd seen on Darlene's face earlier. It could be me.

"I could say it is none of your business, and it isn't." Nyberg stopped while George put a salad and sparkling water in front of him and gave me my coffee and third dessert. "But it's no secret." He reached into his pocket and extracted a slim black wallet, removed a business card, and tossed it onto the table.

I read. Lars Nyberg, CPA, and the name of a well-known consulting firm.

"I'm an accountant. We're doing the audit for the province, preliminary at this stage. Getting a handle on irregularities before we decide our focus," he said.

I felt like a fool, my theme for the day. An accountant. The last thing I expected.

"So you aren't buying property?"

Nyberg shook his head.

"Not hijacking sewing machines? Not bribing politicians? Not sneaking into my house when I'm not looking and making tea?" I stopped, then decided to go all the way and watch his face. "Not murdering anyone?"

"Excuse me. Are you crazy? I think we're done here. This conversation is getting out of hand." His salad was untouched.

The look of distaste on Nyberg's face stunned me. I'd let my nerves get the better of me. "Listen. I'm sorry." I was, somewhat. "There has been a lot of stress in my life lately, and I want it to stop. I really, really need for something to make sense."

Nyberg relaxed, slightly. "I understand. Not quite, but almost. You know, this wasn't what I expected either when they sent me up here. I mean, people dying, geez." Nyberg toyed with his fork. "I'm just trying to do my job."

Good. I needed to move this conversation back to safe ground.

"What exactly is your job?"

Finally, his expression said, *something I want to talk about.*

"This province is full of rural communities, and many of them have been run without any fiscal supervision. Over the years, there have always been rumors and complaints about these small councils. The province wants to clean it up. That's why I'm here."

The expense reports, the road, Harry and Mack—that was probably only part of it.

Nyberg continued, "The other thing is towns this small don't have the tax base to warrant independent councils. To be honest, you probably need development to bring in more revenue. Without it, Gasper's Cove could lose town status and be amalgamated with Drummond."

I shuddered. The folks in Drummond would love that; they already called us "Last Gasp."

Nyberg wasn't done. "Evidence a town's not able to self-govern responsibly would be part of that decision. Documents were forwarded to us which made clear an investigation is necessary."

Gerry's envelopes. Whoever had slipped the information to the reporter was spreading it around. This was bad for councilors like Mack and Harry, and the community itself, but who would have benefitted from it? This was a question worth answering.

My third dessert was finished.

"So you're here only to look at the books?" I asked. "Because someone tipped you off?"

"Primarily. The rest of it, all this turmoil"—he looked pointedly at me—"is not in my job description. To be honest, at this point, I just want to go home."

"Me too," I said. "That's all any of us want."

CHAPTER TWENTY-TWO

After Nyberg left the Agapi, I sat and considered all the ways I'd been a fool. I'd never been good at slowing down, but my mental jump from car-parked-outside-store to monochromatic-man-must-be-developer had been reckless, embarrassing, and inappropriate. In my search for answers, I was batting a solid zero, and worse, I'd been unfair to a harmless accountant. Adding to my embarrassment, I'd even sent some desperate emails to an old acquaintance. I picked up my phone and made the call.

"Julie, sorry to bother you, but it's Valerie. I sent you a couple of emails?"

"Oh, right. I've been meaning to get back to you. Listen. I tried to get some information on that Lars Nyberg guy you asked about. Nothing."

"I know. I'm an idiot. I got it all wrong. Sorry to put you to all this trouble."

"No problem. This gave me an excuse to call up a guy I used to date. He works with strip malls and knows who does dollar store real estate. He told me it was someone called MacKenzie. Does that ring a bell?"

"Not exactly, but I'll check it out. Thanks for the help."

"Like I said, no biggie. Going out Saturday with this guy, so thanks. Take care of yourself up there and good luck."

We ended the call, and I got up and went to the cash register to pay. George waved me aside; Nyberg had paid for my coffee and dessert, which made me feel even more like a jerk. But what could I do about that now? As my mother used to say, if you can't be smart, at least be useful. I remembered then that Duck had told me the crafts were piling up at the back door, and he was afraid he'd knock something over carrying in bags of peat moss and lime. He wanted to move it all to the basement, at least until the space upstairs was ready. The day wouldn't be a total loss if I went over, helped him, and made sure all the crafts I was bringing in were stored out of his way.

When I got to the store, Polly was at the cash register.

"No school today?"

"Nope, another professional day. My parents wanted me to be with them at the office, but it's boring over there, so I came here."

"What are you up to?"

Polly shook her head. "Well, the first thing I did was talk Rollie out of switching over to cryptocurrency. He tried to argue that it was the wave of the future. I reminded him the tide's still out around here. Think he might have got it."

I laughed. What would Polly be like when her chronological age caught up with her head? "Listen, Polly. You were here the other day when that man came in, weren't you? The guy who wanted to buy the store?"

"Yeah, what a loser."

"What can you tell me about him? His name? What he looked like?"

"A short man with brown hair is what I remember." Polly reached down and lifted the cash drawer from the register, exposing a mess of business cards underneath. She shuffled through them, pulled one out, and handed it to me. "Here he is."

Ralph Mackenzie

Real Estate Consultant
5400 Bloor Street W.
Toronto, Ontario

"Not Lars Nyberg."

Polly looked at me. "Lars who? A Viking? Is this something from social studies?"

"No, it isn't. It's a case of jumping to conclusions and not knowing what I'm talking about."

"Got it. Like *A Stranger in a Strange Land.*" She saw the puzzled look on my face. "Science fiction. A classic. 'Is the house white? This side is white.' It's about 'don't make assumptions.' You should read it."

"I will. When my life gets simpler, I definitely will."

After I left Polly, a quarter of my age and already twice as smart, I went off to find Duck. I walked past the row of buckets and pails; the mounds of chicken feed; and the coils of turquoise, lime green, and scarlet hoses, looking for our handyman. I stopped when I heard a voice I recognized. Next to me, in the drywall aisle, Brent Cameron was on the phone. Moving carefully, I tiptoed closer until I was parallel to where Brent was standing. Peering over the pegboard between us, I saw him with his back to me. Concerned I'd be seen, I eased a hinged display of drawer pulls open, blocking his view. Close, but hidden, I could hear his side of the conversation.

"I'm telling you: we can get in touch with the power folks now. Get the installation ready to go."

The back of Brent's jacket shimmered under the store lights. Too much polyester. What was he doing with Darlene? She was silk dupioni.

"Nay, no, don't worry about the council. The warden's out of the picture, and once we have the by-election, I'm going to have someone in there who won't be a problem at all. She'll do everything I say—count on it."

Brent listened, then laughed.

"A hairdresser. Can you believe that? She thinks she could be a warden. I'm serious. Kind of hot, but not a clue about politics. Just what I need, right?"

Pause.

"I know. It's been a real cleanup job for sure, but I think it's done now. I'm not going to let you down. It's the wave of the future and I want in on it. Contact the head office and tell them we've come through with our part of the deal, getting the approvals, and they need to get the power folks on board. Leave the rest to me."

I'd heard enough and took half a step back, stunned. Poor Darlene. To have her hopes raised just to be let down again would be too cruel. It was all I could do to keep myself from throwing drawers of nuts and bolts at that sneaky, crooked, self-satisfied, and self-confident creep in the next aisle.

But I had to do this right, be smarter than that. Going to Darlene now and telling her what I had overheard would be another blow to her pride and dignity. I needed to prove her political mentor was deep into something disreputable and then have her be the one to make the decision. Let that be the reason she dropped him. Darlene didn't need to know how Brent had just described her. I'd never tell.

However, given my success rate as an investigator—I had skillfully unmasked a greedy developer and probable murderer as a homesick accountant—I had to figure out how to get Brent Cameron to reveal his true self. As I watched, Brent put his phone away in the pocket of his over-fitted, shiny suit jacket and walked back into the main area of the store.

I needed help.

What else had Brent talked about besides Darlene? Something about power. Whose power? Then something about land approval. What did this remind me of? I looked up at the store's pressed metal ceiling. Approvals, building approvals, rules.

There was someone I knew who could make sense of this. I needed to go to the town council office. Duck and the crafts would have to wait. It was time to see Kenny MacQuarrie.

CHAPTER TWENTY-THREE

The town offices were quiet when I arrived, but Kenny was in. The front desk clerk was trapped in a phone debate on spring potholes, so she waved me through to Kenny's office, pointing me to the end of the hall. I saw Kenny through an open door, head in his hands, as he stared at an open copy of the Nova Scotia building code.

I knocked on the doorframe to get his attention. "Can I talk to you?"

He looked up at me. "Come to tell me something I already know?"

"I don't think so. What are you talking about?"

Kenny reached into a pile on the edge of his desk, next to a large, framed picture of his drooling but adored old bulldog, and extracted a letter on Province of Nova Scotia letterhead.

"I was copied on the letter they sent to you and the council. They've rubber-stamped the heritage proposal. There's something in it about a new program to preserve the fabric of rural towns. This means more work for me, documenting everything." He was gloomy. "But if you get the beam in, I now have to lift the stop work order on the renovations."

I dropped my purse onto the green linoleum floor and staggered with relief to Kenny's battered wooden visitor's chair. "I didn't know the application had even gone in. How did this happen without Mack?"

Kenny sat up, inflating with the realization he knew something I didn't.

"Mack did it before he, well, you know, went overboard. Signed his form, gathered the rest from the councilors, and faxed them through to Province House in Halifax," he said. "Support from the whole bunch was unanimous. Surprised the heck out of me."

"You're not the only one," I said. "Of course I'm happy, but surprised, too. What about the pro- and antidevelopment factions?" And what about my theory that Brent was in league with the dollar store developers? Or that he might have murdered Mack to derail the heritage bid? Some detective I was.

Kenny picked up the framed picture of Max and dusted it off with his sleeve, repositioning it carefully, as if to protect it. Avoiding my eyes, he straightened up his papers, holding up the piles and tapping them on the desk until all the edges lined up.

"I figure Brent and Harry have some other scheme up their sleeves, something in it for them," Kenny said with disgust, raising an envelope and shaking it for emphasis. "Guys like that always do. They think the rules never apply to them. They don't even know there are rules."

"We can agree on that one," I said, then stopped. The envelope.

Right there in Kenny's hand, with the town's crest in the corner. Where had I seen a big envelope like that recently? On my dining room table. This was an envelope just like the ones that held Gerry's notes and evidence.

Kenny saw me staring at his hand and then lowered it slowly to the desk. He knew he'd been caught.

"It was you, wasn't it?" I asked. "You collected those old expense reports and passed them on to Gerry." I motioned to the open door and the suite of offices down the hall. "You work right here. You had access to everything."

Kenny looked stricken. "If you say anything, I'll lose my job," he said, sweating now, his aviator glasses sliding down his nose. "I'm good at what I do. I had my reasons."

"What reasons? To get back at a couple of rule breakers? Why not just report them to the audit? Why go to the radio?"

"Is that what you think? That I'm some bureaucratic whistleblower? No. Do you think I don't know the procedure? Who wouldn't resent those people?" he asked, voice rising to a squeak. "Mack, especially. He thought the rest of us were just nobodies."

What was he talking about? Then I remembered the yearbooks at the library. Mack, the high school star, and Kenny's picture, with nothing written beside it. Mack, the hockey player, the businessman, and then the town warden. Is that where this all started? Had the slights added up over the years until Kenny couldn't take it anymore? Had he hated Mack enough to kill him?

Down the hall, the clerk was still on the phone. None of this was good. Why had I come here?

"You all went to high school together, I remember," I said. Maybe if I kept Kenny talking, I'd make an opening to leave. I had to get out into that hall, and away.

Kenny nodded. "Yes, we did, and for a while, high school was better. Linda and me in the chess club. I taught her how to play, you know. Then Mack came along, and there was no more chess club. Worse, he ended up dumping Linda for the stuck-up Brent's snotty sister Maureen. Mack and Brent have been nothing but trouble in my life. But that's not why I gave Gerry the files."

Gerry, the link.

"It wasn't?" So far, this sounded like a pretty good reason to me.

"If I tell you something, will you promise not to tell anyone? I want to keep this job."

Good luck with trying to be a building inspector from prison, I thought, but I said the words he wanted to hear.

"I promise."

"Okay, I'm going to close the door," Kenny said, going around his desk and returning to sit again across from me. The room was suddenly claustrophobically small, my cotton spring cardigan too warm. "Gerry was blackmailing me. He wanted more money than I had, so I made a deal. If I'd get him some dirt on a couple of the councilors, he would keep quiet about me." He paused and almost smiled. "I thought he'd use what I gave him to blackmail them, so there was still some justice in it."

Blackmail? "So, why was he blackmailing you? My part of the deal. Tell me," I said, my mind whirled as I tried to process this new development.

"I guess it doesn't matter now. My résumé. I don't know how he found out, but he did. I lied on my résumé. I said I'd graduated as a building inspector when I didn't. I ran out of cash before I could finish the program. I took all the courses at the college I could, then just read the regulations and figured it out," he said, his face a mix of pride and sorrow. "I'm an excellent inspector. I'm well-respected. Gerry threatened to take it all away."

"You finally had power," I said, thinking out loud and then regretting it. "You have the rule book and can shut anyone down." I suddenly understood something. "Hang on. No one called to report us at the store, did they? You made that up. You just came and inspected on your own, didn't you? We were just another chance to throw your weight around, weren't we?"

Kenny stared at me. "What was I supposed to do? It's my job to make sure everything built in this town is done according to the regs, and how did I find out about your little reno job?" His voice rose with outrage. "When I went in to buy Max a new dog bowl. The noise, the dust. Construction going on right in front of my eyes and I wasn't even consulted. Unbelievable."

"Is that all you care about? Being the big authority?" I took a breath and then blurted out my question before my brain could reel the words back in. "That's why you killed Gerry and Mack, isn't it?" Somebody had to be the murderer. Eventually, I had to get this right, but still, I wished the door wasn't closed. "I'm calling the RCMP," I announced recklessly.

"Why? What are you talking about?" Kenny looked shocked. "I didn't murder anyone, and if I inspected your place, I had every right. Calm down. I've already talked to the police. They know where I was the night Gerry was murdered. Don't you know what time of the year this is?"

"Spring?" What was he talking about? Was this the season to kill people?

"*Strix varia.* The barred owl. It's nesting season." Kenny was indignant. Who didn't know this? "I am an audio ornithologist. I record bird sounds. For just a few weeks this time of year, the males call out to their mates. Very distinctive howls and screeches, unique, thrilling. I spent the night in the woods with the rest of the birder club taping it."

"The birder club?" I croaked.

"Yes. We're a large group," he said, holding up a hand, "and before you ask, I didn't kill the warden either. I understand he died out on the water. That lets me out too. I get terrible seasick. It's well documented."

I leaned back in the wooden chair. Owls. I'd never considered owls. I sighed. "Kenny, I guess we're even. You're"—I searched for the right word—"a diligent building inspector. I can attest to that. So, I'll keep your secret. But in return, I'd appreciate it if you didn't spread it around that I accused you of two murders. I've been doing too much of that lately."

Kenny stared at me, pity and maybe a little sympathy on his face. "You're a smart woman, Valerie. I can see that. But maybe you should slow down on trying to figure people out and maybe notice who they are more. It wouldn't hurt."

He had a point. "So, where does this leave us now?" I asked.

"At strictly business, from now on," Kenny said. The building inspector was back, and we were both relieved.

"You and Rollie get that beam up, then call me. I'll come right over. I know you have a deadline."

"Sounds great. We'll be in touch." I stood and moved toward the door, then hesitated, remembering why I'd come. "By the way, if you hear anything specific about something Brent is cooking up, let me know."

Kenny straightened up, alert. "Why? What have you heard?"

"Overheard is more like it. Something about approvals and power. I'm not sure what it's about."

"Interesting." Kenny looked thoughtful. I had his full attention now. "I'll see what I can dig up, but I have to ask: Why does this matter to you?"

"I still think something is going on with that vacant lot between his dealership and the store, and that worries me. But mostly it matters because Brent Cameron is using my cousin Darlene, and I can't let him do it."

A look of understanding crossed the building inspector's face. "He likes to use people, that's for sure," Kenny said. "I'll check it out. Anything to wipe that smirk off that face, I'm in."

"Thanks, Kenny. This is more than I can deal with on my own." Support was coming to me from the strangest places. "Another thing. You know, I wouldn't mind hearing those owl tapes of yours one day. I had no idea there was all that happening in the woods right now."

"There's always a lot going on that most of us miss," said Kenny. "Birds have taught me that."

CHAPTER TWENTY-FOUR

What next?

I'd held my breath waiting for the heritage designation. Now that we had it, the renovations could go into high gear. Rollie and I needed to talk and make a plan, but back at the store, I couldn't find him anywhere. Then I passed his office. The door was closed. Rollie had a client.

My cousin, I knew, was conducting his real business— giving advice. Behind the office door, there would be a man who said he'd come in for a rake but wanted to talk about an interfering mother-in-law, a teenager who wouldn't talk, or a wife who wanted him to do yoga. Working through problems like this would take time. Rather than waiting, I went down to the basement to help Duck with the craft inventory.

I loved the store, but I hated the basement. It was dark and musty. The ancient walls were made of rough stone, and the floor, in places, was still packed earth. Naked light bulbs hung from cords tacked to the beams, and the only additional light came from small windows on the exterior walls, close to the top of the foundation, which were submerged in wells below the level of the street and last cleaned in 1923. When we were kids, we used to dare each other to go down here, fully aware that in about five minutes, whoever we'd sent would be back up, face pale, and blathering about scuttling shadows in the corners and strange moans under the stairs.

Despite these memories, my grown-up mind knew the basement was a logical place to store the crafts. Long benches spanned the room. Above the benches shelves ran floor to ceiling along the length of two walls—a leftover from when canned goods and other staples were stored down there. The shelves were perfect for grouping the crafts so we could begin pricing. I felt guilty that Duck had already done so much by himself, but once I descended the steep stairs, I saw he had two helpers—Shadow the cat and Stuart Campbell.

They'd been busy. Most of the crafts were already neatly arranged on the shelves. They had a system: Duck carried; Stuart organized. I noticed little notes taped to some shelves: "Kitchen-crochet-pot-holders," "Kitchen-wooden-utensils," "Kitchen-decor," "Kitchen-misc."

"I know, I know," Stuart said when he saw me. "My mom was a cataloger in a library. You now have a window into my childhood. I had labeled sections in my sock drawer."

"Stu's been a big help," Duck said. "He caught me wandering around upstairs, just holding stuff. He saved me."

"No problem. It's been fun. I think I'm good at this," Stuart said. "I was waiting to talk to you, Val, so this gave me something to do."

"Well, here I am," I said. "And, by the way, did you hear? This is now a protected property."

"Rollie told me. The bank's going to give him the money, so now we can get the beam in; then you're good to go," Stuart said. "But it's not why I wanted to talk to you."

I felt myself flush, but before Stuart could say anything else, Duck caught sight of Shadow on the shelves.

"Hey, kitten, you get out of there," he said, running over to her. The cat was up on a shelf, calmly batting crocheted pot holders onto the floor, working her way methodically toward the stained-glass window ornaments. When she heard Duck's voice, she paused, stared at him, and deliberately knocked the last pot holder off the shelf, then jumped down, clearly making the point that no one would tell her what to do.

Distracted, I turned to Stuart. "What do you want to talk about? Don't tell me we have another structural disaster."

"No, nothing you don't know about. It's personal. I need a favor."

A personal favor? This was interesting.

"It's for Erin, my daughter. Her birthday's coming up. She'll be thirteen ... a teenager, heaven help me." Worry crossed his face. "What do you get a girl that age? Who knows? So I was thinking, how about a sewing machine? She's really into this crafty stuff. What do you think?"

"I'm the wrong person to ask," I said. "I'm of the generation who thinks everyone should sew; I've been sewing since I was eight. Wearing something you make yourself gives a person confidence. I also think it helps young people establish a sense of identity. Teaches kids they can do things for themselves. A sewing machine's a great idea."

Duck agreed with me. "True, everyone should sew. Real practical. Learned how to do it, you know, when I was … well, you know where I was. We did contract work."

I looked at Duck but held my tongue. Whatever he and Rollie had been up to the night of the ER visit remained a mystery. Plus, whoever had taught him to sew should have done more work on the "don't sew through people's fingers" part. Sensing what I was thinking, Duck, embarrassed, retrieved the cat and went up the stairs, leaving the engineer and me alone.

Stuart watched them go, then turned to me. "But what do I buy? Can you help me?"

"Let me think about it. There are a couple of options, but listen—can we go upstairs? This place gives me the creeps."

Stuart laughed. "It's a bit of a dungeon, isn't it? And there's another thing. The road project we talked about. The fish plant. I found something out."

"You did?" I asked as Stuart let me go up the stairs first.

"Yes, it took some work to verify it, but I was right. By putting the road there, they had to bring a huge amount of fill. And guess who they hired to do it?"

I had a good idea. "Mack?"

"You got it. Council put it out to tender, and his company was awarded the contract. They had the lowest bid, but just barely. It was almost like Mack knew what the quotes from the other companies were before he bid himself."

"Get out," I said. "Are you saying he did a dirty deal on top of a dirty deal? Set it up so the council would approve a job he'd profit from, then made sure he got the work?"

"That's exactly what I'm saying," Stuart said. "It looks like our warden was quite the operator. Not that it matters anymore."

"What do you mean? Isn't this what the auditor is looking for?"

Stuart smiled, but without humor. "That's the thing, isn't it? I checked the terms of reference. The province's audit is only to look at current councilors and members."

"Does that mean what I think it means?"

"It sure does. To be blunt, Mack's not a current member anymore, is he? Now, no one's going to be digging up shady deals from the past. His death saved a few reputations."

CHAPTER TWENTY-FIVE

As I walked home from the store, it occurred to me it was unfortunate that the warden's body had come ashore. I liked my running-away-to-avoid-scandal-but-still-alive theory a lot better. No one should go before their time. As I climbed the steps to my aunt's bungalow, my only home, and none of it mine, it was clear to me that very few of us end up with the lives we planned. Little wrong turns can become big ones; casual decisions can lock the door behind us.

But if we were lucky, the souls who counted on us were also the ones to save us, like Toby and me. He'd been such a good boy today, waiting patiently at the store while I met with Kenny, and then again when I left him to go to the basement, a space he disliked as much as I did. As I let Toby into the house I told him I'd make it up to him, that we'd do an extra-long walk around the neighborhood after dinner.

It was a soft night. By the time Toby and I left the house the evening fog had rolled in, making halos around the streetlights. In the distance, I heard the foghorns calling out to the boats, keeping them on course and safe as they headed back to port. The moody, salty mist in the air made me think of Mack and Gerry, two men with more secrets than ethics, now both gone. Somewhere out there was a third party, a murderer, and whoever it was, chances were it was someone I knew. That thought, like the damp, went right through me.

Preoccupied, I let Toby set the pace and lead me along our walk. As usual, he took his time, but after our usual circuit, we reached the end of the street and crossed. We were almost home.

Our house was the second from the end at the cross street. As we came around that last corner, I had a clear view through my neighbors' trees to our back deck and the door to the kitchen.

A motion caught my eye. Something was up on my deck. Why hadn't I left the back light on? I shortened the leash and pulled Toby in. The shadow moved. What was it? The washing I'd left on the line, moving in the breeze? A hump-backed raccoon looking for food? That wouldn't be unusual. Or was that a figure, a person, close to my back door?

Yes, it was. My throat tightened, closing off my breath. Was this my intruder back, trying to get inside the house again?

I needed to know. Crouching down behind bushes, I pulled Toby closer, and I moved across my neighbors' backyard and up to the garden shed on the edge of our two properties. I ducked behind it. Handing Toby a dog treat to keep him quiet, I carefully, one inch at a time, moved my head until I could see over into my yard.

There he was.

Now that I was closer, I knew it was a man, a hoodie pulled up over his face, bent over near the the door to my kitchen. In his hands was something long and narrow, too wide to be a hunting rifle, but undoubtedly a weapon. The figure moved slowly, closer to the door. I reached for my phone. Afraid to make a noise, I scrolled through until I found Dawn Nolan's number and texted her.

> Someone is trying to get into my back door.
>
> I'm outside in the Davises' backyard. Come quick.
>
> Emergency.

I added that last word just in case.

I got down lower, not taking my eyes off my back deck, and gave Toby another treat, hoping the sound of his crunching wouldn't carry. As my eyes got used to the dark, I saw the man more clearly. He opened a backpack and carefully placed something down by the door. What was it? Explosives? I went still, afraid to move. This was worse than I'd thought. When would the police get here?

Suddenly, a car door slammed, and there were voices. Two flashlights played across the front of my house and then bobbed as they came around the side path to the backyard. The figure on the deck stopped. I held my breath.

"Police. Stop right there."

The man on the deck stood.

"Hey, Wade, how's it going?"

I recognized the voice. Harry Sutherland.

"Harry, what are you doing up there on Valerie's deck?" Officer Wade Corkum's voice was matter-of-fact, loud in the dark.

"Leaving crafts. From my mom. She said to put them around the back. Guess Val's not home."

"Yes, she is," I said, moving out from my hiding place and walking into my back yard. "Harry, you nearly gave me a heart attack. What's going on?"

Harry raised the long package. "A picture, framed. Mom would kill me if anything happened to it. Maybe we should put it inside?"

I was close enough now to see the amused look on Wade's and Nolan's faces; they'd both come out on the call.

"Another nonemergency. I should have known," Wade said.

Officer Nolan was more sympathetic. "False alarm, but Harry, what do you expect? Doing stuff like this at night. What was wrong with the front door?"

"Mom was worried someone might take it. It's *The Last Supper*, in filet crochet. Mom worked on it for nearly a year. And these here," he added, gesturing to the smaller bag at his feet, next to his backpack, "are angel ornaments for Christmas trees."

I reached the deck and took the crocheted art Harry handed to me. Somehow, I was surprised he was such a good son.

Wade Corkum studied the large maple tree above him and shook his head before facing me. "This is the last time, Valerie. The last time. If we didn't have work to do, this would be funny. But we do, and it isn't." He turned and nodded to my deck visitor. "And Harry, next time make your deliveries in the daylight, okay?"

"Will do, buddy. I promise," Harry called out cheerfully to the officers as they walked away to their cruiser. He turned to me. "Well, I guess I'll be going now too."

"Not so fast," I said, opening the back door. "I'm losing my mind here. Someone's got to explain things to me, and it looks like you're all I have to work with. Get in here."

Harry looked like he wanted to leave, but with the air of a man long used to women telling him what to do, he reluctantly followed me into the kitchen.

I took Harry's mother's crochet into the dining room, laid it respectfully on the table, and then returned to the kitchen. I bent down and filled Toby's water bowl and pulled out the kettle. "Tea?"

"I don't drink tea. Do you have coffee?" Harry asked. "If it's not too much trouble."

"Not at all. Have a seat." Pulling coffee from the cupboard, with my back to Harry, I asked in what I hoped was an off-hand tone, "So, what's going on with you and Darlene?"

I turned around. Harry was bewildered. "Darlene? She cuts what's left of my hair. What about her?"

He wasn't getting away with this. "Don't give me that hair-cutting nonsense. Something's going on, and no one's talking."

"Talking about what? You have Mom's *Last Supper*. That's what I came for. I should go." Harry was ready to bolt.

"The casino, Harry. She's the call you made when they threw you out the other night. She picked you up. Don't deny it. I have a witness." I reached down to stroke Toby's solid back to steady myself and waited.

Harry picked up the pepper half of the "Welcome to Niagara Falls" shaker set and studied it intently.

"The casino? You know about that?"

"Yes, I do. You were seen."

"I never called Darlene."

"You did. Someone saw her come and get you."

"Never called her."

I had no patience for this. Harry Sutherland couldn't possibly know just how little patience I had left. I tore the pepper shaker out of his hand and returned it to safety at the center of the table with its partner.

"Then who called her? Why was she there?" My voice was loud and shrill. Toby whined, alarmed. I was scaring him.

"Leave Frank out of it," Harry said.

"Frank? Her uncle? Excuse me." Where did this come from? I sat.

"I slipped. Darlene's uncle Frank is my sponsor. I knew I was getting into trouble, and I called him. He doesn't drive, so he sent Darlene. She's his niece. She knows." Harry looked as weary as I felt.

I put my face down on the table and stayed there. Eventually, I raised my head and stared at Harry; things were starting to make sense.

"I saw the two of you behind the church," I said.

"That would be us, coming out of a meeting. Don't know where I'd be without those meetings and Frank. He knows how it is."

A fragment of the conversation with Darlene came back to me. Some trouble in the past, someone in the family who made a mistake. Had Frank once lost his license for drinking? And then there was Brent shutting Gerry's story down by threatening to pull his ads. But that didn't mean

Gerry couldn't still blackmail the former pastor. The list of people who had a reason to kill Gerry was growing.

"He was blackmailing you, too, wasn't he?" I asked. "Gerry."

"He tried to," Harry said. "Somehow, he found out about me fiddling the expenses. I don't know how that happened." I kept silent and let Harry continue. "I got myself into trouble with money a while back. See, the thing is, once I get going, I don't care. That time everything was good ..." Harry said wistfully, "until it wasn't."

I could hardly dredge up the energy to be sympathetic, not toward someone who had caused me so much trouble, but suddenly Harry looked small and defeated. "But what about Mack? Why did he okay the expenses?"

Harry looked startled. "Mack? It was him? I don't know. I handed in the papers and hoped for the best; they always paid me. Maybe it was because I tipped Mack off about the fish plant?"

"The road? You mean the road?"

"Yeah. Knew from working down there if they built near the water, it'd be a ton more work. Good for him and his trucks. I think Gerry figured it out too. He talked to one of the old truckers."

Neil, wood-carving Neil. I remembered now: he said he talked to Gerry.

"You're telling me he tried to blackmail you, but you didn't pay him?" I asked. It was amazing to me that Gerry found the time to do his radio show with all the blackmailing he had to manage.

"Yes and no," Harry said. "It's complicated."

I got up and poured Harry's coffee. Honestly, his poor mother had been putting up with this for years. Good thing she was a woman of faith.

Harry watched me carry the coffee to the table. "Three sugars and cream if you have it," he said.

I put the cream, sugar, and a spoon down on the table, possibly with more force than necessary. I pulled out a kitchen chair and sat down. I wasn't getting up until I had some answers.

"Harry, I don't mind complicated; everything is complicated right now. Start talking."

CHAPTER TWENTY-SIX

I counted the sugars Harry stirred into his cup. Four, not three. He couldn't even be honest about that.

"Here's the thing," he started. "Gerry tried to hit me up. He knew if everything came out, that'd be it for my career in municipal politics. Of course, I didn't have the money to pay him off, so I went to Brent. Don't know what he did, but that was the end of it."

"Good old Brent," I said. "Helps everyone out."

Harry laughed. "He wouldn't have any friends if he didn't buy them. Wouldn't be anywhere without the old man, and he knows it. So, he bails you out, always there to buy you a drink, but then he has you, and you get in deeper and deeper."

"What do you mean by that?" It was too bad Darlene couldn't hear this.

"You know about the audit the province's gearing up to do?" Harry asked, changing the subject.

"Of course. I met Lars Nyberg; he told me all about it." I was happy to show I knew something about something.

"That's the fella," said Harry. "I knew I would be back in trouble with an accountant digging. So, I talked to Frank. He said to come clean. He told me to own up to it, make amends. It's what we do. Try to make amends."

"Okay," I said. "What did that look like?"

"I made a deal to pay back the extra money I claimed and promised not to run again in the next election. But when I told Brent, he went nuts."

"Why?" I asked. "What did it have to do with him?"

"A lot. Because without me to rubber-stamp everything, Brent would back to square one, power-wise," Harry explained.

My head was spinning. "I don't get it. I thought Brent was all for development, for the dollar store, the increased tax base, things like that. But then you both supported the heritage proposal and shut the developer out instead. It makes no sense."

Harry was surprised. "The dollar store? Brent was never interested in that. He has his own plans for the lot."

"He does? What?"

"I don't know. He wouldn't tell me. But Mack knew; that's why he voted to protect the store. It never had anything to do with you and Rollie. But with Mack gone, and if I'm out, Brent's got to be nervous. He has to control the council to get what he wants. That's where Darlene comes in. She'd be the new me."

The morning after *The Last Supper* had arrived on my deck, Toby and I were up and out early. My conversation with Harry had kept me awake, words and thoughts zinging around my head all night. I hoped the fresh air would lift my mood like it had the early morning fog.

After the fiasco of the night before, I decided we needed a new route, so I put on my red boiled wool jacket and we headed up, not down, the street. This took us past the Smith residence. I noticed a light on already in the basement apartment. Noah must be up early too, no doubt getting ready for work.

That strange hole-in-the-wall rural radio station. It had been a while since I'd thought about my interview, but when I did, I recalled Gerry's clumsy flirtations, beginning with his attempt to remove my headset.

What had he said then? I remembered. It needed to be tightened because Mack and his big head had been in before me. What, I wondered, had they talked about?

Noah would know. I texted him.

> Sorry to bother you. Have a question.

No trouble, what's up?

> Gerry interviewed Mack the same day
> he talked to me. What happened to
> that interview?

Good question. It didn't air. Let me check.

It was much later in the day when Noah got back to me.

"I found the file." The young reporter was excited. "It wasn't in the lineup anywhere, but I found it in a folder of to-be-edits. Gerry's files were always a crazy mess."

"What does it sound like?"

"I'll let you be the judge; I'm sending you the MP3 now."

My phone beeped; Noah's email had arrived. I clicked it open, then listened. With a start, I realized this was a conversation between two murder victims. It was all surreal.

The first part of the interview was predictably boring. Mack droned on about the boat parade and said folks should sign up if they wanted to take part. The last part of the exchange, however, got my attention as I listened to Gerry winding up with a standard question.

"Anything else you'd like to add?"

"Yes, there is," Mack said. "This might be a good opportunity to share something that the voters, including my good wife, who'll enjoy this, should know. Something I've been holding on to for the right moment."

I could almost hear Gerry sit up in his chair. "Go on. We're all ears."

Mack cleared his throat, ready to launch into another monologue. "Well, Ger, getting ready for the parade this year reminded me of how much I enjoy being on the water. I need to give myself more time for my boat." The warden paused for dramatic effect. "So I've decided to retire. To leave politics. Not put myself up as a candidate in the next election."

Gerry let out a gap-toothed whistle. "Mack, this is news. You've been warden a long time. What can the people of Gasper's Cove expect now? Any thoughts on a successor? Who you'd like to see take over to preserve your legacy?"

"I don't want to take sides," Mack said, chuckling because he knew he was about to do just that. "I'd say anyone on council would do a good job, but one name comes to mind: Brent Cameron. He's who I'd like to see run. Brent's shown leadership on council and has a proven track record in the community." Mack was pleased. He'd dropped his bombshell and now, he thought, the interview was over.

Gerry had other ideas. "Hold on. Before you go ... Warden, I have a few questions. Does your decision to retire have anything to do with the upcoming audit the province is undertaking on small-town councils like ours?"

"What do you mean?" Mack sputtered, sounding uneasy.

"How comfortable are you with an auditor looking into the fact your former construction company trucked in and provided fill for the new road out to the fish plant?" Gerry asked, his voice rising faster and louder as he spoke. "How comfortable are you with having expense reports you approved subject to scrutiny?"

There was a moment of dead air. I wondered if I'd come to the end of the recording, but then I heard Mack's voice, the swagger gone right out of it.

"No comment."

Gerry laughed, a mirthless, self-satisfied laugh. He had what he wanted.

I pressed *stop*, stared at the phone in my hand, and then called Noah.

"I listened. What do you think?" I asked. "Was Gerry going to use this to blackmail Mack? Or was Mack the big fish, the story more important than blackmail?"

"Good question," Noah said. "I think he was going to air it. He'd already started to edit. He wouldn't do that if he was going to use it for blackmail. I guess he died before he could broadcast it."

"This is getting stranger and stranger. Every time I think I understand what's going on, I'm wrong. There's always an explanation for everything, except what matters," I said.

"You mean the murders?"

"Exactly. We still don't know who killed Mack and Gerry, or why. But one name keeps coming up, and I've got a feeling he's the missing piece who'd explain all of this."

"Who are you talking about?" Noah asked.

"Brent. Pull out those investigative skills of yours and see what you can find out. Somehow, he's in the middle of all of this. I'll meet you back at the Smiths'; then we can talk."

CHAPTER TWENTY-SEVEN

I went over to the Smiths' house about five-thirty. Joyce Smith met me with a message from Noah.

"He asked me to apologize. He'll call you later—said you'd understand." A small, efficient woman, Joyce treated her basement tenant like the son she wished she still had at home. "Are you busy right now, Valerie? Can I ask you a favor?"

"Of course," I answered. "What can I do for you?"

Joyce wiped her hands on a dish towel. "I was wondering if you could stay and watch a loaf I have in the oven. My granddaughter has gone across to Drummond to her dance lessons without her shoes. Her mom wants me to run them over."

"No problem," I said. "What do I do?"

"Just sit and check it in, say, twenty minutes, and take it out if it's done. It's for one of the older ladies from church. She loves my cherry loaf."

What could I say? There'd been enough drama in the community. The least I could do was to help get one senior her cherry loaf.

"I'll take care of it," I said. "You get those dance shoes to your granddaughter."

Alone in the house, after Joyce left, I looked around. It had been a long time since I had been in the Smith home, but nothing much had changed. There had been some minor upgrades to the kitchen, but otherwise it was still decorated in a style I would call impeccable housekeeping mixed with furniture inherited from dead relatives. If the place had been a car, it would have been described in *Auto Trader* as in mint condition.

The couch and chairs were early 50s. The rug was definitely 60s, but the heavy, dark dining room set had to be early 20s at least. There were white crocheted dollies on the arms and backs of all the seating, and framed wedding photos of various family members, all advertising their shared genetic background with the famous Smith ears.

The only relatively new piece of furniture I could see was a nice recliner much like the one Toby sat on at the store, strategically placed near the front of the picture window. I sat in it as I waited for the loaf to bake. It was a very comfortable chair. I wondered if I should get one for myself since it was likely I would spend the rest of my life alone, and I wondered how much they cost, and if they came in colors other than dusty rose. While I considered these fundamental decorating decisions, I looked through the window and realized with a shock that the chair had been precisely positioned to give the Smiths a direct view of my house. From where I sat, I could see my front door, my picture window, the driveway, and the side door to the basement. No wonder my phone rang whenever I'd left my car lights on or had dropped a mitt in the driveway. The Smith household could watch everything that went on across the street at my place and probably did. They were decent people, but it felt odd. What did they see?

The oven timer went off. I leapt out of the chair and ran into the kitchen, just as I heard Joyce pull into the carport. Quickly, I grabbed a pair of rooster-decorated oven mitts and pulled the loaf out of the oven, not a moment too soon. The edges were starting to brown, and the top had a short crack in it. I put the pan on the cutting board beside the stove and draped a tea towel over the top. The side door opened, and Joyce came up the short flight of stairs into the kitchen.

"Made it," she said. "Got the shoes there before the music started. Can't understand how her mother can drive a child all the way over to dance lessons and forget the tap shoes. Of course, the inside of the car is such a mess, you wouldn't know if you remembered them or not—worse than the house."

"Oh, well, no one runs a house like you do," I reminded her, with sympathy for her daughter-in-law. "I know I couldn't."

Joyce was uncomfortable. "Val, I've been meaning to talk to you. Know how much you've got going on and everything. But if you ever need a home-cooked meal, you can come over here. Ask Noah. I'm a real good cook. No need to get those senior meals delivered."

Senior meals? I was taken aback. By my own calculations, it would be decades before I'd consider myself a senior. "Meals? What are you talking about?"

"I saw the lady—you know, the poor lady who lost her husband—from Meals on Wheels, over at your place. Dropping off a big box once. Like I said, you can eat here anytime."

Joyce's face was kind with concern, but my mind was racing. Maureen McRae. Mack's wife and Brent's sister. The "MM" signature at the bottom of Harry's expense claim. Maureen, her husband's administrative assistant at the council, the helpmate who paid his tab at the store, and now no doubt covering for her brother by entering my house and trying to scare me into silence. How far did her family loyalty go?

"Joyce, don't worry. I'm still cooking for myself," I reassured her. "But I've got to go. Someone I need to see."

CHAPTER TWENTY-EIGHT

After I'd left the Smiths' and headed down into town, I thought of all the people Brent Cameron had used and controlled. The Cameron money and influence helped Harry hide his secrets and helped Maureen and her husband live beyond their means, but at what price? Then there was Darlene. She'd been offered something more valuable than money—respect. To take that away now would be cruel.

I knew what I had to do. I needed to let Brent know I was onto him and get him to leave Darlene alone. It was the only way I'd protect her, and I had to do that first. The rest was up to the RCMP.

But how dangerous was he?

If I met him, it had to be in a public place. The car dealership would be perfect. It was right there on Front Street, with its big windows facing the sidewalk. I'd be safe there.

But when I arrived, the dealership was closed. The "Zero percent financing" flags still flapped in the breeze, and the life-size cutout of Brent himself, hand outstretched, ready to close the deal, was plastered to the window, but the doors to the showroom were locked. It was five p.m. on a weekday in a small town. I'd missed my opportunity.

Deflated, I trudged over to the store. Duck met me at the door, his massive key ring out, ready to close up.

"Hey, Duck. Rollie still here?" I asked. "I wouldn't mind talking to him. I've got something on my mind and I need his advice."

"Too bad—you just missed him. He went down to the Agapi with your engineer friend to talk renovations. Try there." Duck stopped and studied me. "What's going on? You look upset."

"I am. I wanted to see Brent Cameron, but the dealership was already closed."

"What did you want to talk to Cameron about? He and his sister were in here a while ago."

"They were? Doing what?"

"Something for the boat. They're going to scatter Mack's ashes on the water when they get them back." Duck shook his head. "If you ask me, it's kind of weird. Mack goes out on the boat, gets killed, washes in, and now they are going to take him back out again and float him away. They're a strange bunch."

"I don't think any of us knows how strange," I said.

"True enough. Listen. I've got to go. We're out of cat food." Duck pulled his car keys out of a pocket and turned to head for the back door, then paused. "Some more of those craft things came in. Can I leave you to take them downstairs?"

"Sure. Where are they?"

"At the back door. Driftwood lawn ornaments. Tourists will buy anything." Duck shrugged. It made no sense to him why anyone would pay for something they could collect along the shoreline for free.

After Duck left, I carried the pieces through the store and down to the basement. We were running out of space on the shelves. I pushed over some miniature lobster traps to make room for the driftwood. I looked at the rows of shelves. Further down, they were a mess, all the order Duck and Stuart had so carefully established, disturbed. Even worse, dozens of the friendship bracelets the girls had made were scattered over the dusty floor, a sight that both hurt and angered me. Surely Shadow hadn't done all this. Something wasn't right, not right at all.

Suddenly I felt a motion, like a wave, in the air behind me.

I turned slowly.

I was not alone.

Maureen McRae was standing in the shadows in the corner near the giant old furnace, the arms of its ductwork stretched out around her like the embrace of a subterranean monster.

In her hands were a crafter's stained-glass Christmas ornaments. Slowly, her eyes looking right into mine, she dropped them, one by one, to the floor, sending shattered glass everywhere, the sound echoing in the deep, dark space.

"Maureen, what are you doing?"

"What does it look like? I am just making sure this won't happen," she said, gesturing to the rows of handicrafts. "The last thing I need is to have this town in the news, a camera crew coming in, a bunch of tourists."

There was only one way out. I backed up carefully, slowly, to the wall of shelves, nearer the stairs. "You don't have to do this."

She looked at me with surprise. "Of course I do. I had enough. If anyone should understand, it would be you."

"Me?"

"You know what it's like. I know you do. I've been pushed around my whole life, just like you. The difference is I pushed back." She was proud of herself. "My dad used to say I should marry someone who'll keep me in the style to which I would like to become accustomed. That always got a big laugh around the dealership. Like that's all I was supposed to do with my life. Marry. I knew the business inside out. But who did Dad give it to? My idiot brother."

So much for my loyal sister theory. "But you had Mack," I said. "You were a team."

"Shows how much you know," she sneered. "Mack. A big fish in a small pond. I did his thinking for him. I got him elected. I made him warden. But you know what he did behind my back?"

"No, tell me," I coaxed. I needed to keep Maureen's rage focused on someone other than me.

"He fooled around with petty scams, got sloppy, and attracted an audit, and before I could fix it, he decided to retire—went public before he's even talked to me." Maureen snapped a shard of broken glass in her hand. It glinted in the dim light like a knife. "And you know why?" she asked, her voice shrill and cold.

I shook my head, my throat closed too tight to speak.

"The boat. So he could spend more time on that ridiculous boat." She smiled. "I was cleaning his stupid fish, he started talking, and then he was over the side. Not much of a splash."

"And Gerry?" I managed to croak out. I was afraid to ask but had to know.

"His own fault. Gerry started it. Mack told me he'd taped an interview and announced his retirement. He said Gerry knew about his deals too, but Mack wasn't worried. 'If I'm retired, there's no story,' he said. Shows you how many brains he had. Retired, we'd be nobodies."

"What did you do?" No one was as smart as Maureen was, not in her mind. I could see that now.

"I cleaned up, like always. I went to the station to ask Gerry not to air the interview, to let it go. He laughed at me and asked me to leave. All I did was open the door at the top of those stairs." Maureen sighed, satisfied. She'd fixed everything.

"They're going to catch you," I whispered.

She held up the long, broken spike of glass. "I don't think so. I'm ahead of this. I stopped Gerry from broadcasting that stupid interview. I stopped Mack from ruining everything we built." She paused and stared at me, her eyes dead and flat like a fish's. "I'll stop you too."

A small movement behind Maureen caught my eye. There in the corner, at the very tip of Neil Ferguson's hand-made, hand-painted, built-to-scale model of a Nova Scotia lighthouse, in its little window, carefully made and framed with mitered joints, was the tail of a mouse. A store mouse, who, like decades of its ancestors, couldn't mind its own business. There it was, inside an icon, oblivious now to the gray cat, haunches high, nose low, crouched on the rafters above.

I held my breath and kept my gaze steady on the woman in front of me—hair done, eyebrows shaped, makeup perfect, and insanity on her face.

Then Shadow made her move, and with one impossibly acrobatic swoop, the cat leapt down from the ancient structure of Gasper's Cove's only genuine heritage building onto the lighthouse and the mouse.

When the cat pounced, the lighthouse tipped, and the mouse went flying through the air and into the freshly done roots of Maureen McRae's shiny, dark hair.

Maureen shrieked and dropped the glass. If there is one thing that will derail a killer, it is a live mouse in her hair. Every time.

Then, with the instincts and focus of any successful store cat, Shadow, ignoring the screams, continued her pursuit, following the mouse down and onto Maureen's head, until the four of them—mouse, cat, killer, and lighthouse—landed at my feet.

Stunned but at least upright, I took the opening the chaos gave me. Pausing only to reach out and pull the fire alarm on the wall, I ran up the stairs and into the arms of Stuart Campbell, where I stayed until we heard the fire trucks.

The thing about a small town is that when anything happens, everybody comes. First was the fire truck, arriving at top speed from Drummond, followed by RCMP Officers Nolan and Corkum, then Noah, and finally Harry, Frank, and the rest of the AA meeting from the church down the street, no longer quite as anonymous.

Rollie came too, and when he arrived, the firefighters let him go down and see Maureen, who he talked to gently in his therapist's voice until she was moved from the middle of the cold floor where she sat, surrounded by broken fragments of white and red wood, a small blue and white flag stuck to her chest.

And Shadow and the mouse? They were nowhere to be found, their work for the day done.

CHAPTER TWENTY-NINE

Sometime after Maureen's arrest, I got a text from Noah.

Coffee? Agapi?

Sure. Meet you there at 10?

👍

The first thing I noticed when I walked into the restaurant was that Noah had a tie on. He looked older now, more assured, and grown up. I realized his work term was almost over. I slid into the booth across from him and ordered a short black and baklava. I'd be sad to see him go; dessert would help.

"What's been going on?" I started, trying to sound cheerful.

"Lots. I have some news," Noah said. "Interesting news and good news."

I picked up my fork and took a bite. "Like what?"

"I'm doing a feature on Maureen. There's a lot there. The RCMP say she confessed to both crimes. Said she didn't have the energy to lie anymore. The whole story's pretty incredible."

"I imagine it is," I said. "After that horrible scene in the basement, I've been trying to understand. I guess her whole life was spent living through someone else. When that was threatened, she snapped." It could happen to the best of us, I thought.

"There's more to it," Noah said. "It's not that simple. She had her own ambitions. She was going to run for warden, go for the power herself. She knew if Mack retired, she'd probably lose, especially if Darlene ran, but with him dead, she'd win with the sympathy vote. That's what it was all about."

"You've got to be joking."

"I kid you not." Noah was excited, the real reporter coming out. "You know how the police knew Mack's death wasn't an accident?"

"No. How?"

"A propeller. Cut him up. He went overboard offshore; they figure someone started the engine and left him, all when he was trying to get back in the boat. They were just trying to figure out when it happened. Before the boat came in, or if it went out after."

"That's horrible." I was shocked. "But how do they know Mack didn't start the engine himself?"

"No need to that day. Good wind. Mack was a sailor. Maureen wasn't; she could run the outboard but not sail. She also didn't know enough about tides either—or she would have known he'd wash ashore."

I shivered. "She was in my house, that woman—made herself tea in my kitchen. A killer."

Noah looked puzzled. "Tea? I don't know anything about that. A girl I know who works at the police station said Maureen was raving when they brought her in. Something about a sewing machine. About you. How you should have locked your car when you were at a hospital, and that she knew the teacup shouldn't go in the dishwasher. What's up with that?"

I told Noah how Maureen had been in my house, twice.

"That's nuts, completely sick. But it explains something."

"That she knew how to scare me? She sure did that. But why?"

"She was afraid of you. She thought Gerry might have told you Mack was retiring. And she said someone with eyes like yours was dangerous. Does that make any sense to you?"

"It's a long story, and you wouldn't believe it if I told you. Let's say my psychic abilities are unreliable." I changed the subject. "What about Gerry? What happened there?"

"He couldn't stop talking, a hazard of the radio business," Noah started, then stopped when George came to refill our coffees and lingered to catch the conversation. All of Gasper's Cove wanted to hear this. Noah smiled but waited until George left to continue.

"Poor old Gerry couldn't help himself. He started showing off. I understand he told Maureen he had lots on Mack, something about a road, and he knew she'd signed off on Harry's expenses, to bribe him to keep quiet."

"That was what set her off? The fact that she was involved?" It made more sense to me now. "She couldn't run if this came out."

"You got it," Noah said. "Ego and ambition—you never know how much anyone has. Politics brings it out."

"A good line," I said. "You should use it."

Noah laughed. "I am. In my story. I wrote this all up and sent it in. It's going out on the wire on Monday. And I got a job offer. CBC."

"That's great." For him, it was. "When do you start? When do you leave?"

"I'm not going anywhere. CBC wants me as a stringer—you know, to cover the shore for them. I'll be their man in Gasper's Cove if anything happens." He laughed. "I'm not from here, but I understand it. So, I'm going to stay for a while, do some surfing, write a book, and take over Gerry's show. What do you think of 'Noah, the Sound of the Surf'?"

"Love it," I said. "Gerry would be proud."

CHAPTER THIRTY

I had unfinished business to take care of. The banner Mack had asked me to sew had been in the basement for weeks, taunting me every time I passed it on the way to the laundry room. I'd worked hard to get it done, finally resorting to reverse appliqué to make the letters in the words *Set Sail for Gasper's Cove* along its six feet of tightly woven nylon. It had taken me so much time, pinning the bright blue fabric to the front and the paper with the backward letters onto the back, straightstitching around the outlines, and then trimming away the excess blue fabric on the right side before zigzagging around the words. I was amazed it had turned out.

Mack had wanted me to add the year, and his name, but I had resisted, and I was glad now I had. This was a project I had no intention of taking on again, and now I wouldn't have to.

But still, it sat, tainted by its history and the cynical bargain I had made—his support for protecting the store in return for this joyless project—now spread out on the old ping-pong table I used for cutting. Part of me just wanted to bag the banner and get it out of my house. Fold it up and put it out on the curb. But my sewing heart wouldn't let me waste something that had consumed so much of my good sewing energy. So after a while, when Maureen's trial was over and her husband and the radio announcer who crossed her had been laid to rest, I decided the banner needed to go to the yacht club where it belonged.

And off we went on a bright, clear morning, the nylon banner and I, to a small cove on the top of the island where locals and visitors moored their recreational boats. As I slowed down to turn into the chipped stone lane that ended at the marina and the clubhouse, I noticed that the carved sign had not weathered the winter well and would need to be repainted. The truth was, the Gasper's Cove Yacht Club, "Sailors near and far welcome here," was considerably less impressive than the name implied. Locals simply called this place the boat—not the yacht—club, which was probably more accurate, because the only real criteria to be anchored here was that the vessel was for fooling and sailing around, not for work. The fishing boats that earned their keep were moored on the serious side of the island, across the boardwalk at the wharf, next to the causeway and facing Drummond.

Most of the yacht club boats were in the water now, down from the wooden supports where they'd spent the winter on land. They were tied swaying in the light waves, attached to the numbered and faded orange buoys bobbing in the water, at the stern flying the flags indicating where they were from—Canada, Nova Scotia, or the United States—and on the bow the courtesy flags of the current waters, the white and blue cross of Nova Scotia. A few, and these belonged mostly to out-of-province sailors who had not yet opened their summer homes, were still up in the dry dock, most still shrink-wrapped in the white plastic used to protect them during the harsh winters.

I parked and lifted my soon-to-be-disposed-of sewing albatross from the back seat of my car and headed across to the clubhouse, the small two-story wooden building at the end of the wharf, with its wraparound deck up top, opening out from the small bar inside. Next to the bar were the bathrooms, showers, and ancient pay phone incoming sailors might need. Hopefully, there would be someone inside official enough for me to offload the burden of my banner.

The door of the clubhouse had a brass kickplate on the bottom and a single round window like a porthole in it, but before I could pull it open, it swung wide from the inside and almost knocked me over.

Brent Cameron.

The car dealer, and the brother of the woman who had done her best to finish me off with a broken stained-glass ornament, was as surprised to see me as I was him. Here he was, the picture of a weekend sailor right down to his brand-new deck shoes, but with hands that would blister if he ever had to haul in rope. Right behind him was a group of flush-faced yacht club regulars who slapped Brent on the back as they passed, thanked him for picking up the tab, and then moved off as a group, leaving him alone on the deck.

"Oh, hi," he said, recognizing me. "I haven't seen you since the trial. I've been meaning to thank you. Some of the things you said about Maureen's mental state made a difference and helped get her treatment. But killing Gerry, her own husband, and nearly you ... I don't know what to say. I guess I don't know my own sister."

"How could you?" I asked. "She was off in a place by herself—a scary, lonely place."

Brent looked uncomfortable, then pulled his sunglasses out of his pocket and looked past me to a bored young blonde waiting in his SUV, the loud beats of the car radio drifting across the parking lot.

"Got to go. Nice talking to you," he said, then paused when he saw the folded fabric in my arms. "Is that a boat banner? Nice. My grandmother used to sew. Glad to see someone still does it."

Then, with his keys in his smooth hands, Brent hurried past me, his eyes on the girl in the car—his sister, and the tragedy she'd brought to our community, no longer on his mind. I watched him go. One day, when this current girlfriend is just a memory, I thought, Darlene will get what she deserves and so will you, Brent Cameron. I have a feeling.

$$\infty$$

After Brent's SUV had rocked its way out of the lot, I pulled the clubhouse door open and went in. Inside, with Happy Hour over and the man who paid for it gone, the building was now dim and empty, except for Harry Sutherland, who, I was surprised to see, was behind the bar.

"I didn't know you worked here," I said. Was it my fate to spend the rest of my life running into this man?

"Yup," said Harry, "I lucked out. If I'd known all this was waiting for me," he explained as his arms swept around the room at the plaques, race ribbons, and old photos covering the club's scarred walls, "I would have left politics earlier.

Now, I've got two sweet seasonal jobs. Perfect. Boat club manager in the summer and my dream job in the winter. I'm set for life." Harry clearly felt he had pulled off the employment coup of a lifetime.

"What's the winter job?" I asked.

"Driving the Zamboni down at the rink, clearing the ice before every game." Harry the councilperson never looked this enthusiastic. "It takes a lot of skill to drive a big rig like that. Sharp turns and the eyes of the public on you. They also asked me if I'd tighten the little kids' skates before lessons too. It will be a lot but I'm quick and used to responsibility," he added, pulling himself up to his full five feet, five inches. "Plus, not everyone has my people skills."

"I'm sure that's true," I said. "Your mother must be so proud." I wondered how many calls she'd made to get him these jobs. A busy Harry was a more-likely-to-stay-out-of-trouble Harry.

"She is, she is," Harry agreed, still in awe at the way his whole life had fallen into place. "Of course, I'm going to keep staying at the house. The price is right," he said with a wink, "and Mom would be lost if I moved out. Least I can do."

"That's very nice of you," I said. "Which reminds me. I wonder if you could do me a favor too." I lifted the banner and laid it down in front of him.

Harry reached out a respectful hand and spread out the large nylon rectangle so it covered the full length of the bar. "Nice work. Is this for the parade?"

"It was. Mack asked me to make it to put on his boat when he led the sail-by. Not sure what to do with it now."

"I get it," Harry said, folding the banner up and putting it under the bar. "Not to worry. I know just what to do.

We got another member, a retired dentist from Belmont, Massachusetts, who's going to lead the sail now. I'll pass this on to him. He's got a real nice 40-footer. Go outside and have a look. You can't miss it."

Relieved to finally get rid of my burden, I thanked Harry, turned down an offer of a drink "on the house, although won't turn down a tip," and did what he suggested. I went outside to have a look at the last port Mack McRae had seen.

Looking across the water in the bright spring sunshine, I could pick out the dentist's boat easily. It was one of a few that could be called yachts. The rest were either small sailboats, light and cabinless, or old lobster boats, working vessels now put out to gentle waving pasture, in service these days only for evening sails with friends or trips around the island with the grandkids. These modest wooden boats, wide and stable, with an open-backed cabin and a steep drop to the lower gunnel, were all built according to a no-nonsense design developed by boatbuilder Dana Hunter of Tatamagouche, Nova Scotia, just for these waters, and just for this life. Nothing, I thought, is as beautiful as something built by skilled hands with not one detail more than needed, a lesson for every crafter.

The water was changing now, the sun higher, lighting it so it shone. It was time I went home; Toby would be waiting for a walk. I hoisted my bag on my shoulder and was ready to leave when I heard gravel crunch behind me. I turned around. It was Polly.

"Well, hello, "I said. "What are you doing here?"

"Rollie brought me. My folks are out showing property, so Rollie and I are doing his errands. I made him a list and arranged it by priority. Boy, does he need a manager? He was planning to go to the library first, then come here, then pay the utility bill. In that order. Believe that?"

"I probably do," I said. My own plan for the morning involved paying bills last. "I would have thought you'd want to go to the library."

"Listen. I go there a lot, but when Rollie takes me all he does is hang around the information desk, trying to get Catherine to notice him." She sighed. "He has no idea how to approach women. You know what he said to her last time we were there?"

I shook my head, trying to process the idea of my cousin with a secret romantic life.

"He tried to compliment her: 'Warm-looking cardigan. Nice and loose.'" She rolled her eyes. "Give him another twelve or fourteen years and he might ask her out, but I'm not hanging around for it."

"I see your point, but what brings the two of you here?"

Polly looked surprised. "Sails. Rollie's inside the boat house now, getting the ones they can't use anymore. He takes them back to Duck to make bags." She caught herself. "Oh no! That was supposed to be a big surprise. For the grand opening. Duck's been working on them for weeks, you know, in the sewing room after you've gone home."

The ER, the sewing needle in Rollie's thumb. Finally, an explanation.

"They really are cool," Polly continued, "and sustainable materials are consistent with the co-op's brand. You should start to think about online retail. You really should. That's the logical next step for growth. In this economy diversification is key."

"Something to think about for sure," I said, distracted. A streamer of yellow caution tape fluttered around the corner from behind the boathouse. I walked toward it down a small path beaten in the weedy grass behind the dock, increasingly certain of what I would find.

I was right. There it was. Mack's boat, *Slapshot*, partially obscured by scrubby bushes, out of the water and on dry land now, held upright in its wooden supports. The boat had been there a while, with the caution tape and "Do not enter" signs tattered by the wind, and that abandoned look boats quickly get when they are out of the water. I noticed the outboard motor had been removed from the stern, undoubtedly taken by the RCMP to the crime lab. I tried not to think about why. I was suddenly aware that I had a child standing silently beside me, and I started to move away. No need for her to see this.

"Let's go find Rollie," I said. "I'm interested in those sails and Duck's bags, but don't worry, I will act surprised when he shows them to me."

I waited, not sure if Polly had heard me. She stood stiffly, staring at the boat. *I shouldn't have come back here with her. What was I thinking?*

"I saw her, you know, the night Mrs. McRae came in," Polly whispered. "I knew something was wrong when she said Mr. McRae decided to stay on the boat."

"What do you mean?"

"He wasn't on the boat. I was sure of it."

"How did you know?"

"When we walked by the clubhouse I heard the music. The TV was on, *Hockey Night in Canada*, the last game of the season—even I knew that. The Stanley Cup. Mr. McRae wouldn't miss coming in to watch that. No way."

I stared at her. She was right. "Did you tell the police?"

"I tried to, but they wouldn't listen to me. They treated me like a kid. It's my fault they didn't arrest her before she trapped you in that basement." Polly blinked away the tears in her eyes. "It's my fault she nearly hurt you."

No one ever listens to a kid, or a sewing teacher, I thought. *Too bad; we notice things.* I stepped back and looked Polly straight in the eye.

"Polly, listen to me. Nothing's your fault. Don't even think it." I looked at my young crafter and businessperson and I knew I had to say the next thing the right way. Polly was quiet, listening to me. She stopped crying.

"Look at me. I'm fine. Do you know what saved me? This is important."

Polly gave me a half smile now. "The mouse? The cat?"

"They were involved for sure, but you know what really did it? The lighthouse."

"The lighthouse?"

"Yes, the one Neil built. A lighthouse like the ones that kept him safe when he was out at sea. He made it. No one told him to, but he did. You and me and all the Gasper's crafters, we make things. We do it not to impress anyone and not because we have some special creative abilities. We make things, the stuff other people just go out and buy, because we can't help it. It's not about making; it's about trying. That's the part that matters. That's the part you have. So don't you ever stop thinking, and don't you ever stop trying, whether anyone else believes you or not. Promise?"

"Yes, I promise," Polly said. "But one thing."

"What's that?"

"Can we talk about something else now? Like setting up an online store?"

"Sure, but I'm going to have to see some numbers. I need to see what kind of a return on investment I can expect," I said, not exactly sure what that meant. "Can I have a proposal, say, sometime next week, once we've got the grand opening behind us?" I was on a roll now. "Can you have something on my desk by after school Wednesday?"

Polly pulled out a small spiral-bound notebook and a pen and started to write down our appointment, then stopped. "You have a desk?" she asked.

"Okay, it's my kitchen table. Same thing," I said. "Just come over and we can talk. I'll bake."

CHAPTER THIRTY-ONE

I'd been interviewed on the radio but never on film. So, before I went down to meet the *Out and About* crew, Darlene came over to do my hair and makeup.

She took over the kitchen, heaved a tackle box of makeup onto the table, and laid out the tools of her transformation trade on a towel, like a surgeon preparing for an operation.

"You know, I heard from Aunt Dot in Florida," I said. "She failed her driving test. She has to sign up for more lessons."

Darlene laughed. "No surprise there. I've seen her behind the wheel."

"There's more. She's marrying the driving instructor. A retired schoolteacher. She sounds real happy."

"Get out of town. She's a sly one, that Dot."

And I had news of my own. "She's asked me if I want to buy the house, a sort of rent-to-own family deal, so I can afford it."

"Sit," Darlene ordered. "That's great news. You're going to redecorate, right?" She picked up her tweezers and zoned in on my eyebrows.

"Baby steps. But I have a home for the salt and peppers."

Darlene plucked. Apparently, I'd have great eyebrows if they were shaped. "No kidding. Where?"

"Ouch. The library. Catherine says once the bicentennial exhibit is cleared out, she wants something to put on the glass shelves in the reading room. She says Dot's collection is famous, part of local history."

"Catherine? What's happening to Linda?" Darlene asked.

"She got a new job. She's going to work in interlibrary loans at the provincial archives in Halifax."

"Really? I thought she'd never leave Gasper's."

"No one did," I agreed. "But I talked to her and she sounds different. This is an awful thing to say, but Mack's death seems to have freed her from the past. It's like the bitterness has gone—just left."

"Good for her." Darlene studied my face. She picked up a large stick of concealer.

"Don't you think you're overdoing it?" I asked. My face felt as if it was being coated in putty.

"You don't understand lighting. You learn these things when you run for political office," Darlene said, grabbing a large brush. "If you don't want to look washed out under those bright lights, we have to go all out."

"Speaking of your political campaign, what happened with Brent? I saw him at the boat club a few days ago. What's going on there?"

Darlene stiffened at Brent's name. "Nothing. Not that there was ever anything there. Not really. All politics." She grabbed an eyelash curler and ran a French manicured nail over the foam pads. "I've been thinking about this election deal. I figured out two things."

"You did? What?"

Darlene stopped, brush poised above my face. "Well, first, local government is interesting, but it's not half as complicated as the world of hair and beauty. I can do this. Second, I decided Brent was a fake. He doesn't care one way or the other about any of it. Not policy, not regulations, not the budget, nothing. It was all just another chance to show off." She put her hands on my shoulders and looked at me through the portable mirror she'd set up on the table. "You know that man has no opinion on the well-water testing situation at all? Zero. Do you believe that?"

"I'm shocked," I said, to cover the fact I had no opinion on well water myself. "That's terrible."

"I should have known," Darlene said. "He even asked me if I could use my salon discount to get him a hairpiece on the cheap. He was just using me. Men get desperate when they're losing their hair."

"Forget about that guy. Move on," I said. "You'll be a great warden. I'll vote for you."

Darlene stopped and looked at me. "I'm not running for warden. Someone else can do that. I'm holding out. If we amalgamate with Drummond, I'll run for mayor of the whole thing. In the meantime, I'm going to take on one of the sitting councilors."

"You are? Which one?"

"Brent Cameron, of course. That's what I'm trying to tell you." Darlene had a satisfied look on her face. I could almost hear the schemes swishing around in her mind. "It will be a fight and probably a dirty one, but I'm up for it. Sarah Chisholm has already done a word-of-mouth poll. She says my chances are looking good, particularly with women, and men 64–80. They vote."

"Wow! I'm impressed," I said. Never underestimate Darlene. "I want a lawn sign."

"You got it. I'll tell Uncle Frank and Harry. They're my sign crew."

Humming now, my cousin went back to work, scrubbing brushes into my skin with determination. She stepped back, assessed her work, and shook her head. "Contour. We've got to get into the contouring, big time," she said, pulling out four palettes of sticky paint. "Let's see if we can make that nose look smaller."

I let her work, then peered into the mirror. I looked like a homemade Kardashian but knew better than to tell Darlene. "What are you going to do about my eyes?" I asked.

"I've got a plan. The beauty of neutrals, my girl. The beauty of neutrals. When I'm finished with you, they'll both look the same color, even if they aren't." I could tell Darlene was delighted to have the chance to attack my face with her arsenal. "You relax. Think of what you're going to say to these people. You've really pulled something off. Sell it."

◯ᕲ◯

The *Out and About* film crew was larger than I expected. They had driven up from Halifax and it had taken two vans. In one were two camerapeople: a relaxed man about my age with a beard, and a short young woman with Celtic tattoos across her biceps and a nice smile. Then there had been a technical guy who took forever to wire up the upstairs craft space for sound and then covered all the wires with duct tape so none of us would trip, which was thoughtful. There was also a young man who knew Noah from school who came to do lighting and was thrilled to see the large semi-circular window upstairs, because natural light is the best, a fact I filed away for reference in case we ever did this again. Finally, we had an interviewer-type person, a young woman in a suit who we all called Tracey, and then Stacey, until she finally corrected us and told us it was Lacie.

We impressed them and we'd earned it. We'd worked for days at this, getting the co-op ready for the grand opening and the film crew. Many of the crafters came in to help, and between all of us—Duck, Rollie, Polly, Stuart's daughter Erin, and me—we'd moved all our craft inventory up to the second floor and arranged it impressively on the display shelves Stuart and Duck had built. I'd been surprised by Stuart's involvement, but when I saw him working along-side his daughter, arranging her friendship bracelets on a table near the window, I understood.

"Wow! I'm blown away here," Lacie whispered to me just before we started filming. "I knew Gerry, you know—worked with him once. He said he was in exile with the last gaspers." She caught herself and looked at me apologetically. "Sorry about that. You know what I mean. I don't know what I was expecting. Certainly not this."

"Did you think you'd come up here and just find someone selling mittens at the end of the driveway?" I asked. "There's a lot of real talent in Gasper's Cove."

"No kidding. I can see that," she said and moved away to instruct the crew to make sure they caught it all—the quilts arranged on sturdy maple captain's chairs; Tilly's knitted baby sets strung out with tiny clothespins on a line; the carved birds perched on the windowsills, as if communing with the real birds outside; and the fishing rope wreaths and door mats. It was all recorded.

Even I had my turn. With Darlene's carefully applied makeup giving way under the heat of the close-up lights, I was interviewed briefly, as a "woman in business"; then Lacie turned to the crafters, the real stars. As I watched, the videographers sought them out in the crowd, adding the faces of the makers to the story of economic renewal in one small Nova Scotia town. Even Duck, normally so shy, came to life in front of the camera and shared with the viewers the techniques he used to make his bags and wallets from old sails. Harry made an appearance too, lifting his mother's *Last Supper* for all to see and then being suitably sheepish when his mom, who like the rest of the town had come to watch, leaned into the microphone and said her faith kept her going through the ups and downs of family life. Polly and Erin made appearances too, using the occasion to pitch their latest idea, a friendship bracelet subscription service. The crafters were upstaged only by a cameo appearance from Shadow as she stalked across the back of a shot on her way to the window to watch the gulls and Canada geese, pausing only to swipe a knitted ornament onto the floor on her way.

As the filming continued, I stepped back, watched it unfold, and tried to see us all the way visitors and tourists would when this went live. Would they see the characters, and appreciate what a community so used to making something out of nothing could create? Would this be enough for them to decide Gasper's Cove was a place worth visiting, not to be missed?

We worked hard; we deserved to be noticed. Rollie strolled past me, in his element, the store full of people, so many conversations underway. He was, I realized, more a host than a store manager. Tourist traffic would suit him well.

"Guess what?" he said to me as he passed, his voice animated with hope. "One of the crew just asked me where we park the tour buses. The province's lining up arts and craft festivals for the summer. This could be the start of something new for us."

"You got that right," said Noah, joining us as he tucked a business card from the video producer into his pocket. "Tour buses—that's next level. Talk to Brent about parking," he suggested. "Since he owns the lot next to you now, he might give you some space. It's just come across the wire. He finally got approval from Nova Scotia Power to put in car-charging stations in that vacant lot next door, the first in this part of the province. He might still have room there for the odd bus or two."

"Good thought," Rollie said, steering Noah past the display of sea glass wind chimes. "He's over there." Rollie pointed to Brent, who was across the room, smooth in a new sports coat, hair carefully gelled, guiding the young blonde I'd seen waiting at the yacht club through the crowd. "I'll talk to him now."

From schooners to electric cars, I thought, Gasper's Cove was transforming.

I felt someone walk up to stand beside me.

Stuart.

"Good work," I whispered. "The floor doesn't creak anymore."

"Solid as a rock. It pays to keep things up, not let them go," he whispered back. "I hope you learned something."

I was offended. Today was a success; I had delivered. "What do you mean? The renovation?"

"No, more than that. You thought it was too much pressure, all the expectations. You got it backward. You weren't taking care of the crafters. They were taking care of you. That's why"—his arm swept around the room—"all of this is here." He leaned a little toward me so our shoulders bumped. I could smell the salt air in his hair and wondered if he'd been sailing. He looked up. "Good sign, by the way."

He was right. I followed his eyes, past the cameras and the lights, past the microphones and the electrical cords, and read the words Duck had painted late the night before, right across the brand-new beam at the top of the stairs.

GASPER'S COVE CRAFTERS: A COMMUNITY CO-OP.

We were just beginning.

∽ THE END ∽

READER'S GUIDE

Crafting for Murder
BY BARBARA EMODI

1. This is the first book in a series about Gasper's Cove and the crafters who live there. What questions do you hope the author answers in the next few books?

2. Rankin's General Store plays a central role in the story and in the history of Gasper's Cove. Was a generation-old family business an important part of your hometown? Do you think that it is important to keep these businesses vital for new generations?

3. Valerie's outlook on life changes dramatically over the course of the book. In your opinion, what or who was the largest contributor to that change?

4. Would you like to visit Gasper's Cove? If so, who would you like to sit down with for a cup of tea and get to know better?

5. Many of the characters are challenged with some sort of change in their lives. Can you relate to what any particular character was going through? If so, which character and how well do you think they handled that challenge?

6. Did Gasper's Cove itself feel like one of the characters? Though fictional, the setting of Gasper's Cove is steeped in the reality of that region. What aspect of the setting did you find most compelling?

ABOUT THE AUTHOR

Barbara Emodi lives and writes in Halifax, Nova Scotia, Canada, with her husband, a rescue dog, and a cat, who all appear in her writing in various disguises. She has grown children and grandchildren in various locations and as a result divides her time between  Halifax; Austin, Texas; and Berkeley, California so no one misses her too much.

Barbara has published two sewing books *SEW: The Garment-Making Book of Knowledge* and *Stress-Free Sewing Solutions* and in another life has been a journalist, a professor, and a radio commentator.

To keep in touch with the latest adventures of the Gasper's Cove Crafters, sign up for Barbara's newletter at **babsemodi.com**

Cozy up with more novels from best-selling authors...

FROM ANN HAZELWOOD

Wine Country Quilt Series

Door County Series

East Perry County Series

Colebridge Community Series

QUILTING COZIES BY CAROL JEAN JONES

Want more? Visit us online at ctpub.com